SO YOU WANT TO ROB THE BANDIT QUEEN

POST-APOCALYPTIC DJ: BOOK 2

K.C. CORDELL

You obviously have highly discerning taste...

And if this weirdness is right up your alley, then you should definitely sign up to receive updates on upcoming books, behind-the-scene sneak peeks, and various chitchat from the author.

www.kccordell.com/newsletter

Dedicated to you, awesome reader, for picking up this book. Thanks for letting me be a little weird!

1

AS SEBASTIAN YUN twists backward and out of the path of a wickedly sharp ax, he wishes he could say this is the first time a girl he's been amorous with has tried to kill him.

Or that it'll be the last.

Before he can regain his balance, Sweetie, owner of a seemingly endless supply of wickedly sharp axes, lunges toward him. She brandishes an ax in each hand and a smile turned manic with rage.

Sebastian succumbs to the pull of gravity, slamming into the rough surface of the stage below. He rolls, not giving himself the chance to catch his breath. Sweetie slices savagely through the air. Her blade cuts through the empty space where his head had been only a millisecond earlier.

His dark hair may be in need of a haircut, but that trim would've been way too close.

"Wait!" Sebastian tosses up his inexcusably empty hands, placating.

Sweetie pauses. She twirls an ax, the motion fluid and well-practiced. Her weapons are as sharp as her curls and ruffles are soft. She is a breathtaking study in dichotomy.

"You really think you can talk your way out of this?" she asks.

Sebastian offers his most disarming grin. "You said it yourself, I got a talented tongue. Which is why I reckon you wouldn't wanna go and do anything regretful to the wielder of such an outstanding talent."

She cocks her head. "I've had better."

"You're just saying that to hurt me."

"No. The axes are for hurting you."

Sebastian scrambles out of the way. Her blades are a deadly whirl that nearly slices his head clean off.

Around him, everything is chaos. Dozens, probably hundreds, of similar skirmishes have broken out across the vast, decrepit building.

Turns out that when a bunch of rival, trigger-happy bandits are stuffed under one roof, they don't need a ton of provocation to erupt into a melee.

Who'da thunk it?

On the other side of the crowded stage, his traveling companion, Meza, squares off against three rough-looking men. Each one is taller, wider, and more muscled than the petite seventeen-year-old. One blows a kiss as they circle her.

She extends a thick wooden slat before her like a club. As far as weapons go, it's better than the big fat nothing Sebastian's working with but not by much.

Between Sebastian and Meza, Scott Buddy moves with freaky, boneless grace, easily dodging assaults from multiple attackers despite the item cradled in its arm. But the lanky monster boy doesn't fight back. Not a single punch or kick or swipe of retractable claws.

What's the point of secretly traveling with a creature of unspeakable evil if it doesn't unleash unholy hell at times that are convenient for Sebastian?

"Hey, parasite—" Sebastian narrowly avoids a blow that would've deprived him of a left hand. "Now would be a really good time to go all *aaargh!*"

Several bandits come at Scott Buddy from different directions. The sludgebrain leaps clear over the heads of Meza and her opponents and lands on an upright piano. "We are making promise."

"Ain't you heard?" Sebastian says. "Promises are meant to be broken."

Meza, Sebastian notices, is now on her biggest opponent's back, the makeshift club pulled tight across his veiny neck. At some point when Sebastian's attention had been otherwise occupied, she'd dropped her two other attackers.

"We are not breaking."

Sebastian growls in frustration. Why did Scott Buddy have to go and make such a stupid promise?

"YOU GOTTA PROMISE," Sebastian insists.

It's earlier in the day. Before sneaking into the bandit stronghold. Before he and Sweetie get... close. Before Sweetie attempts to give him his much-needed haircut, scalp and all.

Sebastian stands between Scott Buddy and the back door of Her Royal Majesty, his decked-out double-decker tour bus.

"No going all *aaargh!*" Sebastian bares his teeth and curls his fingers to mimic claws, clarifying his meaning.

Where they're going, blending in will be the most crucial part of the plan to get back out alive. Scott Buddy displaying its monstrous attributes would be decidedly noticeable. Especially if it starts eating people.

Also, leading a monster to an all-you-can-eat human

buffet? Not exactly something Sebastian wants on his conscience.

The sludgebrain's eyebrows scrunch toward each other, blue eyes wide. It's a decent impression of a hurt puppy. Scott, the formerly human half of this absurd tag team duo, is particularly good at playing innocent.

"Sebastian Yun is not trusting us?" Scott asks.

"Definitely not."

Nearly two decades on a planet filled to the brim with an alarming variety of vicious, bloodthirsty creatures has not lent itself to a stress-free existence. But nothing has given Sebastian more anxiety than the ludicrous decision to allow a body-snatching, man-eating monster aboard HRM.

That level of constant unease is the entirely wrong vibe for a guy who has adopted a "Don't worry, be happy... at least until you meet your horrifying and gruesome end" life philosophy.

Scott nods solemnly. "We are wanting—"

"Start over." Meza's prompt comes on autopilot. Arms crossed and wearing her usual vague look of annoyance, she leans against a bank of storage cabinets.

Scott nods again and starts over, tentative. "I... *want* trust."

Meza dips her head in approval. The resident monster continues.

"Sebastian Yun's trust is very important. I..." It pauses, making sure to use its words correctly. "*Will... earn* trust. Promise. No going all *aaargh!*"

"And your roommate?" Sebastian says, referring to the thing sharing Scott's body.

"Yes. Buddy too."

Moments later, the three of them—technically four of them? Sebastian still isn't quite sure of the math when it comes to Scott Buddy—pour out of HRM and make their way toward Desperado City, where who knows what awaits them.

···|||||||·····|||||||·|||···

IT'S AFTER THE PROMISE.

And after sneaking into the bandit stronghold.

But before Sebastian and Sweetie get… close. And before she attempts to give him his much-needed haircut, scalp and all.

The marauder on stage claims the attention of the hundreds of gathered bandits.

He sports dark leather with giant spikes that echo his impressively pointy mohawk. A rough, full beard accentuates the angry scars webbing from forehead to cheek. And his glass-breaking vocal register would make Phillip Bailey proud.

It's clear why this contestant chose Earth, Wind, and Fire's falsetto-laden "Reasons."

Standing before his raucous audience of fellow bandits, raiders, and desperados, he sings his heart out, closing his eyes to really *feel* the high notes.

The performer's own crew howl their support while the other crews jeer and boo despite the phenomenal performance. A scuffle breaks out on one of the high floors looming over the proceedings. Someone falls screaming to the deck. A tin mug flies from the audience, clatters against the stage.

The outlaw sings on, the retro mic in his grip amplifying his voice throughout the cavernous space.

A final soulful outpour of runs ends on a cloud-scraping note held for a breathless thirty seconds. Its echo reverberates in the air long after the leather-clad outlaw turns to Sebastian with a look of expectation.

Finally, the audience grows hushed, leaning in to hear Sebastian's pronouncement. After all, he is the judge of this contest.

···||₁|||₁|ₗₗ₁||||₁||₁|ₗₗ|ₗ₁|···

IT'S a short batch of hours earlier.

That is, after Scott Buddy's promise but before the performances and the judge's seat, before Sebastian and Sweetie get… close.

Beneath the unrelenting glare of the sun, Sebastian, Meza, and Scott Buddy have positioned themselves in a small cluster of rock formations. They lay side by side on top of a big ol' boulder, flat on their bellies and squinting at the bandit stronghold in the distance.

Correction. Sebastian is squinting. Meza is hogging the binoculars.

He taps her arm incessantly. "Lemme see. It's my turn already!"

"Wouldn't have to borrow mine if you hadn't lost yours," she says coolly. Not so much as a muscle twitches to hand over the binoculars. Her hair, often a dark, textured cloud haloing her head, has been sleeked down into thick braids running along her skull.

"I did not lose them," Sebastian says. "I just… Look, I had a ton of planning to see to and a short amount of time in which to do it. Excuse me for forgetting to pack my binoculars when I was hard at work, seeing to all the various details."

"Going shopping so you can play dress-up, you mean."

"That was a vital part of the plan!"

"Cloud is looking like fluffy bird."

Correction number two. Sebastian is squinting at the bandit stronghold in the distance. Meza is hogging the binoculars. And Scott Buddy, on Sebastian's left, is stretched out on its back, staring at the lone cloud drifting across the desolate sky and, apparently, imagining its next meal.

Sebastian ignores its comment, tries to ignore his uncomfortable proximity to the thing beside him altogether.

"Don't be a meanie," he tells Meza. "Sharing is caring. I need to see what's going on down there too."

"When I'm done," she says.

"Share Bear would be so disappointed in your behavior right now."

"Am I supposed to know what a Share Bear is?"

"All the cool kids do." Sebastian shrugs and returns his attention to the huge structure sitting on the horizon. "I'll let you figure out what it means that you don't."

To be fair, he might be the only person in the entire broken world who knows anything about Care Bears. Nobody spends as much time as he does surfing the data streams of the past, fishing up old shows, movies, books, and —of course—music.

This encyclopedic knowledge of pop culture from centuries long past is sure to come in handy as they attempt today's impossible task of sneaking into an enormous, dicey bandit stronghold. If anyone has an appreciation for long-dead pop culture, it'll be the cutthroats packed into the den of iniquity below.

Right. And hellions make adorable house pets.

"Is it just me," Sebastian says, "or are there a lot more bad guys here than there oughta be? I know the Black Ravens are the biggest crew of them all, but this here's a lot, right?"

The ridge from which he and Meza observe provides the perfect vantage for scoping out the infamous Desperado City, home base for the largest, most intense crew of bandits out there.

Because, of course, bandits are a thing. As if the hordes of hellish creatures and body-snatching monsters preying on humanity aren't enough. At least most Midlanders don't have enough of anything to be worth most bandits' time. It's those poor rich Feudlanders to the south, with their fertile farms and fancy knickknacks, who suffer from the bulk of the bandits' attention.

As if to prove they're bigger and badder than everyone else, this crew is holed up in some sort of humongous warehouse left over from the days when everyone used to live in automated cities that made everyday life unbelievably easy. Humanity thought they'd built themselves a utopia. At least until those cities turned against their masters. It was the beginning of a worldwide nightmare that's still felt generations later.

Understandably, folks have been giving technology the side-eye since then. Most only make use of what they absolutely must for survival. And even though the AI that ran every aspect of life in the old cities had been disabled generations ago, no one wants to live in the shells of what once was. Call it a healthy dose of paranoia.

But bandits are not generally known for making the best life choices.

The enormous warehouse sits on the near horizon like a blocky mountain presiding over the surrounding wasteland. It's massive. More than a few towns—or settlements—Sebastian has visited could fit inside there all at once. The front of the building is emblazoned with a giant black raven encircled with thorns. It's the mark of the crew that claims this territory.

Meza grunts an agreement in response to Sebastian's question. "More than Black Raven marks on them rides."

Finally, she hands over the binoculars. Sebastian peers through them and focuses on the painted details of the vehicles crowded around the building. "Is that—?"

"The Wild Raiders' mark." Meza confirms what Sebastian's eyes are telling him.

Parked haphazardly all around the massive building are hundreds and hundreds of those distinctive bandit vehicles. The black-and-red trucks, motorcycles, and ATVs are adorned with demon horns, bloody fangs, and rotting skulls—both real and painted.

Bandits pimp out their rides with one goal in mind: scare the living ghost out of anyone who spots them as they emerge, roaring, from a furious dirt cloud on the horizon.

A large swath of vehicles share the same symbol. A screaming skull engulfed in flames. Some painted sloppily. Some stenciled. Each of them mean the same thing—the second biggest bandit crew is in attendance.

"What's going on down there?" Sebastian says. "Black Ravens and Wild Raiders hate each other. They can't cross each other's territory without all hell breaking loose."

"Look over there." Meza pushes the binoculars in a new direction.

"Those are—"

"Bashers."

Their mark—a big wooden bat with barbed wire wrapped around it—announces their presence as clear as day.

"Well, ain't that fun," Sebastian says. "It would appear that they are having a little shindig. So now, instead of just one, we gotta sneak into a place filled with the three biggest crews in all of existence. I'm so glad we decided to steal a valuable piece of Old World tech from bandits today."

"*You* decided to steal from bandits," Meza says. "You. The endless source of insane ideas."

"Not all crazy ideas come outta my head." To make it clear exactly what he means, Sebastian sends a significant look to his left.

And turns just in time to see Scott Buddy ripping a

bloody mouthful out of a fat buzzard. The splatters of blood sizzle on the rocky sun-heated surface between them.

Sebastian twists away. "Oh, gross. It's doing it again!"

"Leave them alone," Meza says. "They gotta eat. Just like everybody else."

"It's eating all the time. With its mouth open right in my face."

Scrunching his nose at the pool of blood inching toward him, Sebastian makes the short jump from his perch. He lands in the shade of the surrounding boulders.

"Somebody coulda warned me I'd have a front-row seat to the most disgusting show on earth when I agreed to *your* crazy idea of harboring a freakin' man-eating, body-snatching creature of evil. Ow!" He rubs the stinging spot on his shoulder where Meza has just kicked him.

She glares down. "They ain't evil. Not either one of them. You'd better stop calling them that."

Despite himself, Sebastian blocks the overbearing sun with a hand and peers up at the sludgebrain contentedly chomping away. He'd rather not witness this casual butchery but can't seem to bring himself to *not* look.

"When did you even catch that?" he asks. "You were lying there empty-handed not two seconds ago."

Scott Buddy's red-stained lips stretch into a proud grin. "We are being very fast. Very good hunters."

"Well, that don't send tendrils of terror down my spine or nothing."

Sebastian can't help but recall a much-too-recent memory of being hunted by several sludgebrains. Sludgebrains who were, in fact, bosom buddies with the very one sitting before him.

Of its own accord, his hand finds the blaster at his hip. He doesn't unholster it, but lately, he's been taking extra comfort in knowing his NX-84 Waster is always close. His eighteen-inch FT-K Devastator, currently strapped across his back, is never far away either.

Scott Buddy looks way more human than it had when Sebastian and Meza first encountered it. Regular showers, daily combing, and well-fitting clothes have gone a long way. Now, by all appearances, it's a goofy fifteen-year-old-ish kid too skinny for his height and too pale for the sun-battered Midlands.

No one would think that when that boy had been a small kid, a slimy puddle of goo crawled into his head and turned him into something that spent the last decade or so devouring and enslaving humans.

Helping a sludgebrain blend in with normal people doesn't make Sebastian feel great. But at least he'd gotten that promise out of it before they left HRM.

Scott Buddy's gaze drops to the small, bloody corpse in its hands. Its dirty blond hair falls into its face.

"We are knowing we are eating too much. We..." It presses its lips together and sends a fleeting glance toward Meza before dropping its eyes again. "*I* am sorry."

Sebastian is pretty sure that means Scott, the original tenant of the headspace that is now a double occupancy, is the one talking.

Both halves of the sludgebrain have trouble with the basic concepts of tenses and singular pronouns, but Scott actually makes an effort to get them right, clumsy as that effort may be. Sebastian isn't sure that Buddy, the haughty parasitic squatter, has ever condescended to use "I."

"Buddy is coming out less and less," Scott says. "I am having control always. I am not liking it."

"Whoa, whoa, whoa!" Sebastian pushes his own too-long hair out of his face. Usually, his dark strands are pulled up in a neat-ish, messy-ish bun thing. But today, letting it hang loose is part of the plan. "You ain't telling me that you're sad 'cuz the parasite who body-snatched you as a child ain't running the show for once in your life. You should be celebrating your newfound freedom. Hell, I'll pour you a drink myself."

A sludgebrain host having any control is not the norm. Before meeting Scott Buddy, Sebastian hadn't known that such a relationship between infester and infestee was even possible.

When the other sludgebrains learned of Scott and Buddy's secret arrangement, they took exception to what—among those monsters—is highly taboo behavior. To say they didn't approve might be the understatement of the year.

"Not parasite," Scott says. "Buddy is good. And friend. I am worrying. Very much. I am wishing Buddy is talking to me."

"I don't understand…" Sebastian waves both hands in Scott Buddy's general direction. "I literally don't understand any of this. But if I gotta spend this much time around a sludgebrain, I'd much rather have the part that used to be human running the show. So stay in hibernation as long as you want, Buddy. You hear that?"

"Shut up, Sebastian," Meza snaps.

"Like you weren't thinking it."

Avoiding the vulture blood, Meza scoots closer to the sludgebrain and sets a hand on its shoulder. "This gotta be awful hard for Buddy. It left behind all its friends and family—"

"Do body-snatching monsters have friends and family?" Sebastian asks.

"Leaving behind everything you know ain't easy, no matter who, or what—" She directs that last word toward Sebastian. "—you happen to be."

"We are having to leave because of me," Scott says.

"*For* you. Buddy don't regret leaving to keep you safe.

Never will. Ain't gotta know either of you long to know that. We all do whatever it takes to look after the people we care about. Even when it's hard."

A tiny smile pulls at Scott's lips, and then it blossoms into a wide grin showing off ragged rows of too-sharp teeth. Scott is like an oversized puppy. It's never just a little sad or a little happy. It flies fully in one direction or the other and wears all of its emotions like a big, shiny pin on its chest.

Sebastian points at the horrifying grin. "You better not flash them things when we're around other folk. They're liable to kill us all if anybody figures out what you are."

Scott's hands fly to cover its mouth. When it smiles again, it's with normal, human-looking teeth.

Sebastian turns his attention to the monster whisperer beside the sludgebrain. "And why ain't you ever that nice to me, Meza?"

She rolls her eyes down to Sebastian. "You look ridiculous." All notes of warmth and kindness have left her voice.

"See. That there is exactly what I'm talking about. And I look like a badass."

"You mean a jackass?"

Scott chuckles.

"I meant what I said, woman."

"Can you even move in them pants?"

Sebastian's ensemble can be summed up in two words.

Black leather.

Because everybody—except Meza, apparently—knows that black leather is the very height of bandit couture. They probably don't even know that other materials and colors exist. So Sebastian isn't taking any chances. Boots, pants, shirt, jacket. He's literally got this covered.

Although, he'd had to pull his ensemble together on short notice, so some compromises were made. Not like he had time to shop around. The black leather jacket he managed to barter for has fringe dangling all along the inseams of the sleeves. Not exactly in step with his personal brand, but he's decided he likes it.

The shirt… well, it's more of a man's crop top. Like, super cropped. Like, did they run out of material, and that's why it barely comes past his nipples? But he's pretty sure he's seen bandit dudes in shirts like this before. Plus, with the strap of his Devastator's holster across his chest, it sorta comes together just right.

Besides, he's totally ripped and owes it to the world to show off his hot bod more often. And if he's being honest, the pale skin of his torso could use the opportunity to catch up with his tanned face and arms.

Sure, the pants are just a teeny bit tighter than he'd prefer, but again, short notice. He did pretty good, considering.

"As always," Sebastian says, "I move with the grace and precision of a panther stalking its prey."

Meza stares at him in a way that tells him he's an idiot without her having to say the words.

"At least I made an effort," he says. "Even Scott Buddy put on the vest I found for it."

"I am also looking like badass." Scott straightens the studded black vest it wears, smudging bloody fingerprints across the fabric, but where they're all going, that'll probably help sell the look.

Sebastian gestures toward Meza, looking just normal in the same sort of thing she always wears. Just-normal mechanic coveralls over just-normal shirts and shorts. The top half of her coveralls is currently tied around her waist by the sleeves. "You call that a disguise?"

"Call it not dressing like an idiot."

"Have you ever even seen a bandit? I'm telling you, this is how they dress."

"You got a gallon of sweat dripping off you."

Sebastian stops himself from wiping at the deluge collecting on his brow. Admittedly, heavy, unbreathable leather is not the best material with which to plaster oneself in sweltering heat.

"Here's how it's gonna go down." He snatches his messenger bag from where he'd plopped it onto the ground and tosses the strap over his head. "We sneak into Desperado City. Me and Scott Buddy successfully blend in 'cuz we are totally pulling off these looks, but then you get us caught 'cuz you ain't put on that black strappy number I picked out for you."

"Gonna faint from heatstroke before any of that happens," she says flatly.

"Whatever. Let's get this over with. Upon further consideration, I reckon this whole bandit-convention thing is gonna work to our advantage. Sneaking in there will be a breeze. And since my disguise is flawless, I'll pretend to be the new guy learning the ropes, which will allow me to casually ask a few questions about how things work around here. I'll get my Sherlock on and figure out where they keep the good stuff. Then we grab that gorgeous arm and get out before anyone even notices it's missing. Easy peasy."

···||||||||·|··||||||·|||···

LATER.

But not much later.

It's after sizing up Desperado City from a distance but still before the performances and the judge's seat, before Sebastian and Sweetie get… close.

Sebastian stretches his empty hands high above his head.

A group of scowling bandits press in on him. They wield an alarmingly creative variety of weapons. He is admittedly intrigued by what appear to be two wheels studded with pointy bits and attached to each other by a length of wire, but he would rather not see its use demonstrated.

So, surrender, it is.

"Easy, easy," Sebastian coos to the violence-prone men and women then to himself. "Easy peasy."

2

Well, not before *everything.* Obviously. Not before civilization was screwed three times over. Nor before mankind built the utopia that preceded this current nightmare. Not before television audiences wondered who shot J. R. nor the invention of sliced bread nor the rise and fall of dinosaurs nor the formation of the universe.

So let's say "before all the relevant things."

Before all the relevant things, Sebastian is trying really hard not to lose his breakfast as the creature known as Scott Buddy rips another mouthful out of a poor, helpless rodent. Fur and all.

Somewhere far, far, far back in his mind, there's the thought, *At least it's not biting chunks out of a poor, helpless human.* But that doesn't make it any easier to watch.

Meza, of course, remains unperturbed by it all.

She's behind the wheel, eyes glued to the unchanging landscape ahead as Her Royal Majesty rambles down the dusty road, nothing but desert and faraway plateaus in any of the windows. The passenger seat is swiveled to the side so that Scott Buddy faces her as he munches away, which gives Sebastian an unwanted, perfect view of the sludgebrain's table manners.

Sebastian had chosen this spot at the kitchenette table right behind the driver's seat because it allows him to keep an eye on Scott Buddy. Meza completely lowers her guard around that thing, like she's forgotten that it's a terrifying, bloodthirsty monster.

His holo-interface hovers before him, all but forgotten. He's supposed to be working on a playlist of music curatorial genius for a future broadcast of his show. He's thinking of calling it "We Got You Covered" or "Six Degrees of Awesome Covers."

"Aww…they are being very cute!" Scott Buddy enthuses around a mouthful of flesh and fur. The animated image on its holo-interface—a small group of fluffy ducklings walking in a row—is indeed very cute. Sebastian doubts that would stop Scott Buddy from gobbling them up one by one if they waddled across its path.

"Don't get distracted, Buddy," Meza says, ever the dutiful teacher.

"We are being Scott."

"We?"

"*I* am being Scott."

"Since when?"

"Since Buddy is getting bored with baby animal book." It frowns. "But Buddy is coming out today. For a little. Good, yes?"

"Fine. Don't get distracted, Scott. Read."

"There are six ye… yellow!… baby ducks," Scott reads, then takes another giant happy bite of the rodent. It doesn't wipe at the red dribbling on its chin or trickling down its arm.

"Watch it, sludgebrain!" Sebastian snaps. "You're getting

blood and viscera all over that good upholstery. You can learn to read in a week, but you can't remember how to use a plate and napkin?"

Scott shrinks into itself.

HRM lurches to a stop, the suddenness of it slamming Sebastian into the table before him. When he straightens, Meza is twisted around in the driver's seat with a look that would freeze the sun.

"Scott is trying," she says. "So's Buddy. You got a helpful suggestion, say it in a way that don't make either of them feel like crap. Otherwise, keep it to yourself."

Sebastian gestures toward the mess that is Scott Buddy. "But it—"

"The end." She spins around, and HRM starts forward again. "Go on and read the next page, Scott."

Scott Buddy hadn't been traveling with them a full day before Meza sat it down and explained that Scott and Buddy would have to learn to blend in with humans. It would be dangerous for all of them if anyone discovered that HRM's latest occupant is of a monstrous persuasion. On that, she and Sebastian agree.

Cleaning up Scott Buddy was only the start. Every day, she drills it in walking, sitting, and even standing still like a human. And that's in addition to her grammar lessons.

Maybe the unique way it speaks won't immediately cause anyone to drop everything and scream "Monster!" but Meza declared that the less attention it draws, the better. Reading as much as it could would help it get a better feel for how humans use language.

But it turned out Scott Buddy couldn't read. At least not English. Sebastian hadn't realized until very recently that sludgebrains could carry on conversations or had their own language. They could have tomes of sludgebrain poetry somewhere out there, for all he knows.

In any case, Meza immediately added reading lessons into the mix. Sebastian can't say she isn't thorough. Figures that a girl who, for some reason, can't stand kids would get all "big sisterly" for a pet monster.

For its part, Scott Buddy has taken to Meza's lessons with gusto. Its eyes are almost always glued to a holo-interface, memorizing words from the lists Meza gives it and practicing phonetics.

Sebastian has no idea how long it's supposed to take someone to learn to read, but he's pretty sure it's coming along quicker than average. The tutoring only started a couple of weeks ago, and it's already reading full sentences. Simple sentences, but that counts.

The only thing worse than having a monster on board is having a smart monster on board.

Scott casts a self-conscious look down the aisle toward Sebastian then swivels its seat forward. It reads the next page but much more quietly.

If it were human, Sebastian might even have felt bad.

With an indignant huff, Sebastian flicks his wrist to dismiss his holo-interface and rises. His plan to escape to the upper deck and give himself a break from playing nice with a sludgebrain—because this really *has* been him on his best behavior—is cut short when he spots a town on the horizon.

Instead of moving toward the back of the bus, where the narrow spiral staircase leads to the top deck, he's at the front cab in three long strides.

It's an ordinary, unimpressive town no different than any other ordinary, unimpressive town.

"Nope." Sebastian shakes his head, vehement, gripping the back of the driver's seat as the town comes into better view. "You can keep on driving right past that there."

"Sebastian Yun is not wanting attention from strangers?" Scott says.

"Ha!" Meza says, tone bone dry.

Scott's eyebrows shoot up, as if unsure what it could have said to make Meza laugh. It seems to have asked the question in earnest.

"Are you implying…" Dark clouds gather over Sebastian as he watches the town creep closer, but he keeps his tone light. "…that I am an attention whore?"

"Oh!" Scott's face reddens. "That is not… We are not meaning to—"

"I am," Meza says.

"Well, you are wrong. I happen to appreciate the quiet and solitude of the road. Why ruin it? We ain't gotta stop at the first place we come across."

"We literally do." Meza spares a glance away from the road to aim a pointed look at Sebastian. "You insisted on passing the last two towns we came across."

They live a happily aimless existence aboard HRM, drifting from place to place and accountable to no one but themselves. And their basic needs.

Trading is a big part of keeping Sebastian in the good life. The towns and caravans they come across tend to have useful things, like food and water, to supplement what he and Meza are able to produce and collect themselves. Thanks to HRM's storage bay full of scavenged and refurbished tech, Sebastian and Meza can usually scrounge up something people are willing to barter for.

"What was I thinking?" he says. "Marching the monster you just adopted into an unsuspecting town is obviously the thing we shoulda done."

"That your plan? Keep Scott and Buddy locked in the bus? Never let them interact with people?"

Sebastian frowns at the sludgebrain in question. "You say that as if it ain't a viable option."

"Gotta stop," Meza says. "Need supplies."

"Fine. We'll stop at the next town. Not this one."

"Ain't willing to run out of food 'cuz you got a thing about Hopefuls."

So there is one thing about this ordinary, unimpressive town that's different from all the other ordinary, unimpressive towns. But it isn't the town itself. It's the collection of barely discernible blue flags waving above an encampment some distance across from that town.

Realizing how hard he's grinding his teeth, Sebastian loosens his jaw. He turns away from the view before he pulverizes his pearly whites down to bloody nubs.

"I ain't got a thing about freakin' Hopefuls," he mutters.

"That why you always barrel past a town if them flags're nearby?"

Scott peers at the horizon. "Meza is meaning flags with the white circles?"

"You can see the little circles from all the way back here?" Sebastian asks, momentarily distracted.

"We are seeing. Very clear."

"Of course you are," Sebastian grumbles.

"Why is Sebastian Yun not liking flag humans? Very bad, yes?"

"I ain't never said nothing about not liking them," Sebastian snaps. The tightness in his chest is decidedly not backing him up on that claim.

"They ain't bad. They just..." Meza pauses, considering her words.

"Ain't got a single working brain cell between them." Sebastian marches away from the conversation. If Meza's determined to make a stop here, he'll be in his room, surviving on 2NE1 and Super Mario Bros. with the door barricaded until they're back on the road.

But the HRM is large, and the aisle leading from the front of the bus to the stairwell connecting the two decks is long.

It gives him plenty of time to hear the rest of the explanation.

"They're compassionate," Meza tells Scott. "Hopefuls believe in compassion over all else. Above their own well-being, it seems. They offer aid to anyone asking for it. A place to belong, even."

"This is why Sebastian Yun is not liking?" Scott asks.

"Plenty folk share his attitude about Hopefuls."

"But…" It hesitates, confused. "They are sounding very nice. Good."

"Sure, but folk around here ain't too fond of strangers. Neighboring towns do business with each other 'cuz they know each other. Might trade with familiar caravans. Other than that, townsfolk stay cautious about who they let in. Even then, it ain't for an overnight stay."

"People are letting Sebastian Yun and Meza in all the time." True fan that it is, Scott knows all about their travels.

"It's the show. Folks listen. Feel like they know us. Wouldn't let us in, otherwise. Stranger could be dying outside their gates and begging for help. Town wouldn't let them in."

Meza lowers her voice. At the back of the bus, his foot on the first step of the compact staircase to the upper deck, Sebastian shouldn't be able to hear what she says next. He doesn't *want* to hear her say the words. But thanks to his stupid, excellent hearing, he catches them anyway when she says…

"'Cuz of flatliners."

Sebastian goes cold, freezes in the tight staircase.

He reminds himself that it's only a word. Not even a spell or summoning. Merely saying it out loud won't bring them to his doorstep.

Look at him.

He's almost as bad as those anti-techers and their irrational belief that looking at a piece of technology will draw the ruthless, cunning monsters to them.

His already-tightening chest squeezes even more.

He can't talk himself down as quickly as he usually would. It's seeing those damned blue flags. They've got him all messed up.

Because the past is an asshole.

Whether a guy wants anything to do with it or not, it's always there. Eating the last of the ice cream, leaving wet towels on the bathroom floor, and talking through the best part of every movie. Generally overstaying its welcome when it wasn't even invited in the first place.

"Folks can't tell a flatliner from a normal human," Meza continues quietly. "That don't stop Hopefuls from welcoming anyone who comes across their path. Even strangers. Maybe especially strangers. 'Cuz they ain't got nowhere else to go."

"They are not knowing if they are welcoming flatliner," Scott says. "I am seeing. Very scary for humans, yes?"

Sebastian's laugh is humorless, harsh.

"Even the monster gets it," he calls out from the stairwell. "So why don't those geniuses?"

He abruptly remembers that he wants nothing to do with this conversation, with the idiotic Hopefuls or their stupid blue flags. He snaps his mouth shut.

But in the next second, he catches a case of spontaneous masochism and bursts out of the little stairwell. He, apparently, has more to say, even though this topic is the conversational equivalent of jabbing a knife into his side and twisting it real slow.

"Maybe," he shouts up the aisle, "maybe you can explain to them idiots how flatliners look human, and they're real good at acting human, but it only takes letting one of them in, and then it's already too freakin' late. Then explain how they ain't normal evil like you and your kind, monster boy.

Nah. They're a special breed. You know what? Save your breath. Ain't no use trying to explain common sense to people whose brains are clearly broke beyond repair."

Sebastian makes his leave once again, and this time, he's going straight to his room. He's done. He is not turning back.

He turns back.

"And tell me this," he demands, stomping toward the front of the bus. "What good is all that 'hope' when the monster they let in slaughters everybody in sight? Except the kids, of course. Those, they steal. And we never really know what they do with them kids. Not for sure. They're just gone. Like they ain't never existed."

Scott blinks up at Sebastian with wide eyes. Meza says nothing.

Sebastian crosses his arms, avoids looking through the windshield. "Not that I care about how any of them throw away their lives. But I figured some of us could use a reminder as to why stopping here would be an extremely terrible idea."

"Sebastian Yun..." Scott hesitates. It fiddles with something in its hand. The rodent's tail? *Gross.* Sebastian, momentarily distracted by a sudden gagging sensation, is caught off guard when Scott finally spits out its thoughts.

"We are sludgebrain," it says, "but we are not being evil. Maybe we are finding good flatliner?"

It looks toward Meza as if hoping she'll back him up. But even Meza, the girl who befriended a thing like Scott Buddy, knows Sebastian's right. She remains silent, eyes on the road.

"Like hell," Sebastian says. "And we ain't plopping ourselves down anywhere near the Congregation of Hope for the same reason towns make them pitch their tents so far away. It ain't worth the risk."

"Gotta stop for supplies," Meza says evenly.

"No."

"I am wanting to meet Hopefuls," Scott says. "If Meza is saying yes."

"Definitely not!"

Meza shrugs. "Vote is two to one."

Sebastian stabs a finger toward Scott Buddy. "Since when does that thing get a vote?"

"Since I said so."

"Are we having two votes?"

Meza ignores Scott's question. "The risk is low. Even if there is a flatliner in this camp, their goal is to be invited into towns, but they know that takes time. Plus, they strike at night. They'll be on their best behavior."

"Whatever. Go hang out with your *Hopefuls*." Sebastian infuses the name with all the derision a single word can hold, and then some. "Tell 'em what you are, Scott Buddy. I'm sure they'll welcome you with open arms."

"Really?"

"Not really," Meza says quickly.

This time, when Sebastian pounds his way up the spiral stairs, he doesn't turn back.

If he could, he'd bend all of time and space to avoid going there—not just the Hopeful camp on the road before them, but that dark, tucked-away place in his mind. He'd bury it at the end of a maze so twisted and tangled that anyone who tried to find it would get lost a million times before ever reaching it.

3

Much later.

It's after sizing up Desperado City from a distance but still before the performances and the judge's seat and before Sebastian and Sweetie get… close.

Sebastian stares up at the tallest woman he's ever come across, regretting every decision he's ever made in his entire life. Because it's those decisions that led him here, so close to Ruthless McTaggert that he can make out the surprising hazel of her eyes.

It's way too close. The bandits surrounding her seem to agree.

That must be why they leap to their feet, snatch his blasters away, and point a startling array of weapons at him.

"Easy, easy," Sebastian says, hands shooting upward in surrender. "Easy peasy."

Then again, maybe he doesn't have to regret every decision he's ever made. Just the one that solidified Scott Buddy as a regular fixture in his life. Sebastian isn't sure how monster boy screwed up everything this bad, but the current predicament could only have been its fault.

He makes a mental note to never again underestimate the pure destructive power of an idiot.

BEFORE UNDERESTIMATING the pure destructive power of an idiot, Sebastian is outside of Desperado City. He stops just short of stepping into the reach of its massive shadow.

With so many trucks and ATVs and motorcycles crammed around the enormous building, he, Meza, and Scott Buddy had little choice but to thread their way on foot through the disorganized sprawl of bandit vehicles.

They still have a way to go before reaching the building's entrance, but even from this distance, the open front gate roars, spilling the combined shouts and jeers of countless voices.

From their perch on the faraway boulders, the humongous rectangular building had been a sleeping giant. But the stronghold grew taller with each step toward it. This close, it's a hungry, colossal titan risen up from the earth. Anyone dumb enough to enter its eager maw uninvited will be chewed up, digested, and left on the side of the road for someone to step in.

Despite his air of unreasonable confidence, Sebastian isn't completely clueless.

He knows there are a million ways that sneaking into a bandit fortress to locate and then steal a high-tech prosthetic arm can go wrong.

Rather than feeling the intimidation rightly due the imposing structure, Sebastian is mostly annoyed. He presses his lips together and glares up, up, up at the dark, looming edifice and tries to not think about all the other things he could be doing today. The list is extensive.

But there's something else. Something feels... off.

He turns an irritated, accusing look on Meza.

She narrows her eyes right back at him. "What?"

"This is insane," he says. "You know who's in there?"

She doesn't deign to respond, but Scott looks up at the building and back to Sebastian. Its brows scrunch together as if it's trying to puzzle out a trick question. "Bandits?"

"No, not just bandits. According to legend, the Bandit Queen has spent the last ten years eating up the smaller crews, taking their territories and bandits for herself. Making her the biggest, baddest non-monster thing out there.

"There are only two crews left that come close to posing a threat to her, and only two other bosses still standing against her. I'd bet Her Royal Majesty's cooling system that all three of them bosses are in there right at this moment."

"Just now realizing that?" Meza says.

"We're talking Blade," Sebastian continues. "The crazy bastard who wears the severed ears of those who ever dared cross him on a string around his neck. I mean, how unhygienic is that? And what about El Oso Loco? Who, by the way, keeps the meanest, nastiest hellions he can find as pets. Then has the nerve to give them names like Fluffy and Snuggles. His idea of fun is watching them eat people who disagree with him.

"And let's circle back to the queen herself, the Dread Lady of Desperado City, Ruthless McTaggert. She has terrorized the Feudlands so relentlessly that countless warlords been sending armies and assassins after her for the past two decades, and she is still standing strong. Against, like, *all* the warlords!"

A few Midlanders revere bandits as some sort of larger-than-life heroes. Regular post-apocalyptic Robin Hoods. But Sebastian has never been so naive as to believe overblown tales about noble thieves and reluctant cutthroats. Bandits prey on Feudlanders more than they do Midlanders as a result of simple economics.

Feudlanders have more cool things than their northern counterparts. Way more. The marauders' preference for raiding their southern neighbors is not out of feelings of kinship or solidarity with the poor, downtrodden Midlanders.

Bandits are terrible people who do terrible things. And not because they have to. There are other ways to survive. They do what they do because they want to. Anyone with a lick of sense would stay well out of their way.

"If we get caught," Sebastian says, "they ain't exactly gonna be throwing us a parade."

"Reckon you knew these things before we made our way down here," Meza says, unimpressed with Sebastian's crew-boss breakdown.

"As did you," he counters, "which begs the question, what is wrong with you?"

"Me?"

"Why ain't you trying to talk me out of this? Usually, you'd be telling me I'm a moron and getting all bent out of shape, trying to stop me from doing something really dumb."

"You want me to stop you?"

"Maybe?"

"Sorry to disappoint."

"You don't sound sorry at all."

She shrugs.

"Why today, of all days, are you suddenly Miss Everything's Cool, Go With the Flow?"

She watches him silently. When she looks away from him

and toward the mammoth building ahead, Sebastian is sure she isn't going to answer.

"First I ever seen you do something for somebody else," she says.

Sebastian waits, but she offers no further elaboration. He considers her a moment. She stares back, stone-faced.

The realization jolts through him. "You *approve* of this nonsense?"

She shrugs again. "Other than your ridiculous clothes."

Sebastian sits on this revelation for a moment. It's the first time she's ever approved of one of his outlandish schemes. He isn't sure how to feel about this lack of opposition.

"Hmm…" He hums, pensive. "Nope. I do not like this. It's weird."

She rolls her eyes. "Always making things more complicated than they gotta be."

"Don't you go getting it in your head that I'm a bleeding heart now."

"Never crossed my mind."

"And don't expect me to feel bad when your little hopes of me being some selfless do-gooder come crashing down in the face of reality. This here's a one-time deal. I ain't here 'cuz I want to be. I ain't got no choice."

She crosses her arms. Impatience edges into her cool expression. "We doing this?"

"As long as we got your expectations all straightened out." Sebastian plunges into the vast shadow cast by Desperado City, leading the way forward. "And if you ain't careful, Meza, you're gonna lose your shining reputation as the responsible one."

Expectations firmly straightened out, Sebastian refocuses on the task at hand, only slightly less irritated. This is going to be a pain, but at least it'll be easy as long as he's able to follow the simple and straightforward five phases of his plan.

Phase One: Get inside.

And with so many different bandit crews gathered in one place, slipping into the mix can't be all that complicated.

Phase Two: Look busy enough that everyone thinks he belongs there but also just a tad frazzled, like he's a newbie still trying to figure out how to do his job.

That phase only gives him the tiniest pause. But bandits must have jobs among themselves. Right?

Phase Three: Convince someone that his newbie job requires access to wherever it is they store their stolen goods.

He figures the arm is being kept in some treasure room. Hopefully, they don't do something weird with their goodies, like bury them pirate-style. Although… he would not scoff at the chance to live out a *Goonies*-style adventure. But what are the chances that bandits are capable of that kind of fun?

Phase Four: Retrieve the arm, sneak it out, and make a clean getaway before anyone notices it's missing.

This is the trickiest bit of the plan. If things go wrong here, they'll *really* go wrong. But he's sure he'll figure that part out. He suspects the prosthetic arm will be tucked away in some hidden area of the stronghold, which will give him some options for remaining unseen while he grabs it.

If it's out in the open, that'll be a different story. But no way will something like that just be lying out in the middle of everything.

Phase Five: Do a little dance.

Because they'll have successfully stolen from the Bandit Queen.

Completing Phase One, getting inside, is ridiculously easy.

The stronghold is four times longer than it is wide, with

the entrance cut through one of the narrow ends. Though "narrow" here is entirely relative. Whatever the Old Worlders originally moved in and out of this building must have been ginormous. The entrance is nearly as tall as the building itself.

The gates must have once opened to the entire width of the building face, but whether by choice or faulty function, the entrance is now a slim strip only wide enough for a vehicle the size of HRM to drive through. Sebastian guesses that the gates won't close any farther. The bandits have filled in most of the opening with what appear to be large scraps of metal, leaving a roughly thirty-foot-high gap at the bottom.

Around this entrance, clusters of bandits huddle over a game of dice that elicits shouts each time the little cubes land. A second group cheers and taunts a pair of men who appear to be attempting to kill each other with their bare hands. A few stragglers are in pairs or small groups carrying on boisterous conversations. All seem to be drinking.

Getting past these eagle-eyed lookouts is as complicated as walking in a straight line. Most of the guards hardly give Sebastian and company a glance. The two who look up give drunken nods.

For a moment, Sebastian worries that Scott will be a problem. It walks stiffly and so close behind Meza it's practically in her boots. It stares openly at the guards as if they're exotic animals on display. But no one stops them from entering.

And just like that, they're inside, and it's time for Phase Two.

Phase One was pretty anticlimactic.

If Sebastian weren't trying to get this all over with as quickly as possible, he might be disappointed.

Within its walls, the noise of Desperado City hits

Sebastian in full as his sun-contracted pupils adjust to being inside.

Beside him, Scott winces. "So very loud."

Which marks the first—and mostly likely only—time that Sebastian has ever agreed with a monster.

Whatever's happening here, it has these bandits riled up. He can't make out what they're saying, but their raucous roar is at a fever pitch. He can already guess what degeneracy these cold-blooded raiders get up to.

They're probably watching a bloody, public execution.

Or maybe some melee-style caged death match.

Or maybe they're letting one of El Oso Loco's hellions tear some unlucky victim to pieces.

One can never underestimate the cruel tastes of people like this. But something gives him pause.

"Is that..." He hesitates, sure he's hearing wrong. "Piano music?"

Figures that these people would have music accompanying whatever awful thing they're up to. Live torture must be one big show for them. He wouldn't be surprised to find a concession stand and souvenir booth up there too.

Something large looms ahead. Even as his vision grows accustomed to being indoors, the enormous shape remains inexplicable. It towers high above his head. While it rises higher than the protective walls around any of the towns he's visited, it isn't nearly as tall as the building itself. But this isn't a wall. With a curved form that narrows at the bottom, whatever it is wouldn't stand upright if not for the braces he makes out in the gloom beneath it.

Twin cement ramps, wide enough to accommodate trucks, slope upward on either side, connecting the entrance to an upper level as high as the top of the mysterious curved form. They choose a ramp at random and make their way up.

Each spike in the undulating roar of the crowd puts

Sebastian more on edge. Anything these thugs get excited about cannot be good. These heartless raiders are capable of evils Sebastian can't even begin to imagine.

At the top of the ramp, Sebastian comes to an abrupt stop and gapes. He momentarily forgets about the bandits or even what he's come here for.

Somehow, seeing the building from the outside had not prepared Sebastian for the yawning industrial interior. The scale of it is mind-boggling. The place is huge in a way that transports him to a time and culture long gone.

But that's not what brings him to a dead stop.

In the center of the long, long structure sits a behemoth of the past so massive Sebastian never could have truly fathomed its size without seeing it for himself.

"It's a skyship," he breathes in disbelief.

Sebastian has seen vids and pics of Old World cloud cruises as he waded through the data streams. Skyships like the one before him now, were floating cities where the party never ended and guests could forget their everyday woes.

Though what woes those pampered denizens of the past could possibly have had is beyond him. They didn't have to worry about man-eating monsters or merciless bandits or whether the girl they liked would live long enough to show up for a second date.

Seeing vids of old skyships hadn't prepared him for encountering one up close and personal. Sebastian is in awe, despite it being clearly unfinished. The half-constructed cruise ship had been abandoned by its builders, presumably around the time the crap hit the fan and humanity found itself facing cascading apocalypses.

It looks like somebody took a giant knife and cut the top half of the vessel like a cake, giving him a cross-section view of its many levels. He counts at least twenty. And each level is crowded with rowdy, shouting, and—by all appearances—

inebriated bandits who seem determined to carry on the ship's intended purpose of nonstop partying.

A deck stretches out before the stacked floors of revelry. Sebastian's not exactly an expert on the subject, but he's pretty sure this front deck is twice as long as decks should be. At least, compared with what he's seen of the skyship in vids. He guesses that's the result of the ship being unfinished.

The very front of the deck, closest to where Sebastian stands, is cluttered with vehicles in various states of disrepair. Some have been completely stripped down to nothing but the frame. Others have been reduced to dissected and scattered parts. This vehicle graveyard takes up half of the too-long deck.

Past that, Sebastian makes out the top of a long, tall patchwork curtain. The vehicles and curtains block what's happening on the other side of the deck. But whatever's on the other side of that hanging fabric has captured the bandits' excited attention.

"Phase Two," Sebastian says, a reminder that he's supposed to be finding an opportunity to look like he's hard at work as a newbie bandit. He needs to figure out how this place works.

He continues up the extra-wide, extra-long cement walkway running along the length of the skyship, puzzling over what might lie on the other side of that curtain. He leads the way around rivet-studded steel columns browned with age, industrial clutter taller than they are, and unidentifiable detritus obstructing their path. He hasn't made it far when he realizes Scott Buddy is no longer with them.

Panic flashes through him as he pictures the monster hunched in a dark corner, tearing into its victim, feral with bloodlust.

Of course, Scott Buddy caves to its sick appetite the first chance it gets. Until two weeks ago, the creature's core diet consisted of human flesh. Those cravings don't switch off like a light.

Not that Sebastian cares about any of these merciless bandits getting killed by a monster. But he'd rather not be responsible for it.

When Sebastian frantically retraces his steps to find Scott Buddy, it's standing in the same spot at the top of the ramp where they'd all paused to take in the unfinished party ship. It stares upward at the seemingly endless number of bandits carousing on the unfinished decks. Its mouth hangs open.

"What're you doing? C'mon!" Sebastian snaps.

"So very many," it mutters. "So very many humans."

"Yeah, yeah," Sebastian says. "This place is lousy with them. Keep it moving."

"So very loud. And wild. Very, very wild."

Before today, Scott's exposure to free humans had been limited. This, apparently, is enough to short-circuit its crowded brain.

Meza places a gentle hand on the monster's shoulder. "You'll be fine. Stick with us."

Finally, Scott tears its eyes from the layer cake of bandits and refocuses on Meza's face. It swallows, nods.

Sebastian frowns at the odd exchange.

Scott tends to be bashful compared to the puddle of sentient goo it shares its brain and body with. Not surprising considering how the aforementioned puddle of sentient goo is usually the one running the show. But this isn't just shyness. Maybe even not just intimidation.

It's almost as if Scott is scared.

Of humans?

Ridiculous.

Despite its youthful appearance and puppy dog demeanor, Scott is a monster. And not the adorable kind that cartoon kids catch in little balls.

Shaking his head, Sebastian continues forward. He refuses to get dragged into whatever this is. He has plenty on his plate without adding "play life coach to a sludgebrain" to the day's agenda.

He, Meza, and Scott Buddy aren't the only ones loitering on the walkway. Intoxicated bandits amble across their paths. One not-quite-discreetly relieves himself in an area Sebastian is almost sure isn't designated for that purpose.

A pair of bandits stumble around a thick, riveted column and collide with Scott Buddy. It nearly jumps out of its skin. Worse than that, it nearly jumps out of its human appearance, pink fingers elongating and sprouting dark razor-sharp claws.

"Hey!" Sebastian says, throwing his arms out wide and drawing the attention of the two bandits away from the monster in their midst. Behind them, Meza grabs Scott and pulls it behind a large piece of rusted equipment.

The bandits grimace at Sebastian.

"You're in my way," says one of the bandits, his breath reeking of alcohol. He scowls, revealing teeth sharpened to points.

Sebastian resists the urge to run his tongue over his own teeth, and maybe even manages to keep a funny look off his face.

"Sorry, sorry," he says. "I'm… new here. But don't you worry. I'm working away as any newbie bandit should. In fact, hows about I help you fine gentlemen with some of your chores? You know, blade sharpening or… leather… shining. Or…"

He draws a blank. He really has no idea of the inner workings of bandit crews. Hopefully, these guys can give him some ideas of how to look busy here.

"Why're you still in my way?" Mr. Pointy Teeth says.

The second bandit, a skinny guy with scars crisscrossing his skin, punches Mr. Pointy Teeth and laughs.

"Go easy on him," Mr. Skinny says. "The kid's eager to prove himself. Nothing wrong with that."

"Don't like him. Too much pep."

"Reminds me of you in the early days."

Mr. Pointy Teeth's grimace deepens into a frown. "I wasn't never that… smiley."

Sebastian purses his lips, destroying his grin.

"I know you think you gotta earn your place here, kid," Mr. Skinny says, "and you do, but save it for tomorrow."

"I hear you," Sebastian says. "But you know what's way better than tomorrow? The day before tomorrow."

"Ain't nobody getting any work done today. It's a special occasion. Enjoy the day off. You ain't gonna get another one for a long, long time." Laughing, Mr. Skinny claps Sebastian on the back.

Mr. Pointy Teeth growls—literally growls—at Sebastian as they shove past him.

As Sebastian watches them go, he's only mildly dismayed. The bandits can't really be taking the day off, can they?

"It's okay," he tells himself. "The plan can still work."

He's still wearing his badass leather disguise, which worked beautifully. Those bandits didn't question his being here. If blending in is half the battle, and fives are always rounded up, then Phase Two is basically complete.

Sure, Phase Three is to convince someone that his newbie bandit job requires him to access wherever it is they store their stolen goods, so this whole "day off" thing isn't great. But he'll find some other, non-work-related reason to casually ask someone where they keep their loot.

He's not worried at all.

Meza and Scott emerge from their hidden spot. Scott, at least, isn't sporting claws or fangs, but that was too close.

Sebastian opens his mouth to lash out at Scott, but Meza slams him with a "don't start" glower.

Something tells him he's going to regret not leaving that monster locked in HRM.

But there's nothing he can do about it now, so he lets out an angry huff and continues down the walkway. The piano music gets louder as they move forward, closer to its source. Sebastian makes out a painful screech.

"Geez," Sebastian says. "They're torturing somebody over there within an inch of their life, and the sickos are doing it to… to…" He pauses, verifying that he has at last identified the tune. "Janis Joplin."

He really doesn't want to see someone getting tortured. But with all the bandits crowded onto the skyship, there's got to be someone he can convince to talk. So he can't exactly avoid witnessing whatever's happening over there. In a few feet, they'll be level with that curtain, then a few steps after that, they'll be able to see what's going on.

He stops and turns to Meza.

"We gotta prepare ourselves," he says. "These people are the very worst that humanity's got to offer. They might be breaking someone's bones one by one over there. Or on their fifth hour of waterboarding. Or forcing some poor soul to watch *Cats*. Or maybe it's something I can't even imagine, 'cuz when it comes to butchery and cruelty, bandits have no limits. So I can't tell you what we're about to see, but I know it's gonna be bad."

Thus steeled to see something he'll never be able to unsee, Sebastian continues forward.

When he finally takes in what's happening on the other side of that curtain, he stops in his tracks. All words abandon him as he struggles to make sense of the scene before him.

The curtain serves as a backdrop to a large stage. There's

even a second set of curtains, currently open, at the front of the stage.

On that stage, a woman clutches a mic and does unspeakable things to "Piece of My Heart." It's so bad that Sebastian's ears barely register the auditory assault as an attempt at singing.

"Lord, won't you buy that lady some singing lessons?" Sebastian mutters. "But more importantly, what is going on here?"

"Don't matter what they're doing." Meza blandly takes in the surreal sight before them, as unflappable as ever. "Don't change why we're here."

"Right. Of course," Sebastian says. "We did not come here to sightsee. Stay focused, people. It's just that this is not at all what I imagined bandits got up to in their spare time. Did you? Did you?" he asks Meza and Scott in turn.

Meza declines to respond. Scott shrugs.

Sebastian scratches his head. He's unable to turn away from the awful performance but somehow manages to drag his thoughts back to the task at hand.

"We're gonna hafta switch things up," he says. "This ain't a normal day in bandit land. I get the feeling ain't nobody gonna be talking shop today. And trying to search every inch of this place obviously ain't gonna cut it. You see the size of it. It'll take forever to—"

"I am finding!" Scott chirps.

"Huh?"

Sebastian cranes his head toward Scott's voice, and then his heart promptly skips a beat. Scott has made it halfway up some large rusted-metal framework.

Sebastian has no idea when it happened. One minute, it had been on the walkway with him and Meza, and then suddenly, it's up there.

He swallows a spike of anxiety. It's not outside the realm

of possibility for a human to climb up there, and so far, no one has been paying them much mind. It's unlikely anyone has seen how quickly or easily Scott got up there. Sebastian sure didn't.

"I am finding," Scott repeats.

"I appreciate you being a team player and all," Sebastian says with an impatient tone that isn't very appreciative at all, "but you won't spot it like that. This ain't a *Where's Waldo?* book. Like they'd leave something this valuable lying out in the open. Things ain't never that easy."

"No, I *am* finding."

"Tense," Meza says, mildly.

"I..." Scott tilts its head, thinking. "Found. I found it." It extends a long finger toward the deck.

"What?" Sebastian squints in the direction it indicated. "Where?"

"Next to angry woman in big chair."

Sebastian finds the woman in question. "Oh. That is not great."

Across the crowded deck, only a handful of people are seated. They're spread across three separate raised platforms, giving those lucky few the best view of the stage.

Those are VIP sections if Sebastian has ever seen one. Which he hasn't. But he's heard about them in rap songs and watched actors lounge in them on TV shows.

On the center platform, in what is indeed the biggest and most intimidating chair in the place, sits a woman with what appears to be a permanent scowl across her face. She's wide and tall with pale, short-cropped hair. Additional seating on the platform is filled with more spectators, but none of the others have the gravitas of the woman in the center of it all.

"Well..." Sebastian says, eyes finding what Scott has pointed out, "things just got a little harder."

On a table at this woman's side lies the very marvel of

Old World tech they're here for. He wouldn't have spotted the prosthetic arm on his own. From this distance, it's hard to make out, but now that it's been brought to his attention, he's sure of what he's seeing.

"I reckon," Sebastian says, "that angry woman is none other than Ruthless McTaggert herself."

He's never seen her in person, but descriptions of her have made their way across the Midlands, along with whispers about her reputation. Spoiler alert—she isn't called "Ruthless" for nothing.

He needs a new plan. And fast. Because they have to steal that arm right out from under the Bandit Queen's nose.

4

Sebastian stumbles out of the town as its keepers swing its gate shut. The sun sits low on the horizon. It'll be another hour before dusk gives way to full dark.

The ground is doing that thing where it decides it doesn't want to remain level, choosing instead to swing a little this way and then, nope, time to swing back that way. It's not an unpleasant sensation.

The town, Vigilance, is a decent size. Big enough to accommodate Her Royal Majesty for the night. And unlike the reception Hopefuls receive, Sebastian and company would have been welcomed inside the town's walls for the evening.

The townsfolk certainly treated him well this afternoon, freely sharing their precious bottles of the magical elixir that, sure, burns as it goes down but makes all the less-fun parts of life feel oh-so-very far away.

But Sebastian isn't even comfortable having Scott Buddy locked inside of HRM overnight while he and Meza sleep, or at least attempt to, in Sebastian's case. No way is he letting that creature spend the night inside the walls of an unsuspecting town.

For what it's worth.

He's seen Scott Buddy scuttle up the side of HRM like it was nothing. The walls of a town are much taller than the bus, but would it really present a challenge to a starving and determined sludgebrain?

Great. Something else to spend the night not sleeping on.

The lights of the bus guide his steps, which are only slightly wobbly, thank you very much. (But what can he do when the ground refuses to hold still?)

The sun had still been high when Meza took Scott Buddy into town. Sebastian had stayed behind.

From his room—ahem, *master suite*—above the driver's cab area, Sebastian watched through his window as the two of them traipsed into town. Scott's steps were nervous and bouncing next to Meza's sure and steady march. Sebastian's stomach twisted as they disappeared through the smaller of the town's two gates.

He blasted his music and dove into a version of Super Mario Bros. he'd stumbled upon while exploring the data streams. It had been a part of some Old World project to recreate 8-bit video games. He'd been ecstatic to discover that the games were still playable, and this one in particular promptly became his obsession of the week.

But that afternoon, he couldn't concentrate on it and kept losing Mario to the same Koopa Troopa under the same question box in the same level. Maybe if he kept his eyes on his data cuff's holo-interface *more* and glanced out his window at the town's gate *less*, poor Mario wouldn't have come to his tragic end every thirty seconds.

Finally, Meza and Scott Buddy reemerged from Vigilance, arms loaded with supplies. Sebastian breathed slightly easier.

So, the monster managed to get in and out of the town without slaughtering anybody. Gold stars all around.

Sebastian stayed in his room while they dropped off the supplies. Even when they came upstairs for a moment, Scott Buddy chattering away, Sebastian kept his door shut tight. Then they left again, this time headed for the Hopeful encampment erected far enough away from the town that none of the nervous townsfolk would come out with torches and pitchforks.

Sebastian turned away from the window. But he could see the flags clearly in his mind, waving eagerly from the top of their portable walls as if they thought they could tempt him inside. He heard them, too, snapping in the wind. He recalled the sound easily, no matter how much he didn't want to.

He reminded himself that there were dozens of Congregation of Hope caravans out there. There was no reason to think this one carried her...

Turning up his music, he bounced around to the electronic hip-hop beat and did a really bad job of singing along to CL's rap solo, only able to jump in on the occasional bits of English.

It was somewhere around minute forty-seven of Sebastian showing those stupid blue flags with their stupid white circles that he didn't care about them and, in fact, wasn't thinking about them at all, that he begrudgingly faced facts. No matter how much he very purposely didn't stare at them, he could not make them disappear by sheer willpower.

It was about as likely as him shaking sense into Meza, who somehow, some way didn't have an issue hanging out with those idiots and their apparent dreams of martyrdom.

Then again, she also makes friends with sludgebrains. At this rate, she'll be coming back with a hellion on a leash next, asking if they can keep it.

Emerging from his room with a sudden burst of antsy

energy, Sebastian flew down the stairs and out of HRM. He spent the rest of the day enjoying the hospitality of the good people inside the walls of Vigilance, where no one from the congregation was allowed to follow.

So here he is now, maybe a little more unsteady on his feet than ideal while out in the open of a monster-filled wasteland. But it's not like he has to cross a vast, hazard-strewn obstacle course to reach the safety of HRM. Just a few measly steps in a straight line.

That's not too much to ask for, brain.

The bus is dark, save a glowing window on the lower deck that someone must have forgotten to turn off. Everything appears still and quiet. Meza and Scott Buddy haven't made it back yet. He'll worry about her later. Although he knows that if it gets dark before they return, the Hopefuls will insist on rounding up a group to escort them safely home.

For now, he's relieved he can sneak inside and back to his room without having to endure a lecture from Meza about his current state.

Responding to his touch, HRM's back door unlocks and swings open. The cool air of the bus greets him as the door seals behind him. The narrow, spiraling staircase to the top deck promises to give him trouble. The bastard. But he won't give up so easily. He's so close to his bed. He can already feel his pillow against his cheek.

The musical jingle of clay beads draws his attention.

It's another sound he knows too well to forget. Once, it had been part of the soundtrack of his childhood, but then it became *her* sound.

Even before he looks, he knows who he'll see rising from the couch in the lounge area to his right.

Grace Panya hasn't changed much since the last time he saw her only two years ago. Except for the multiple strings of blue and white beads around her neck. She used to only wear the one necklace.

Her round face, sun-kissed with a smattering of freckles across her nose, is as open and vulnerable as it's ever been. She looks at him with a mixture of nervousness and hope so delicate it might blow away.

Sebastian is frozen, stuck with one foot on the bottom step and his heart ripping itself to shreds in his chest. A part of him wants nothing more than to throw his arms around her.

But the bigger part of him still hasn't forgiven her.

"Nope," Sebastian says and continues up the stairs.

She, like everything else he needs to push away, can remain buried beneath a warren of distractions and misdirections.

5

THE THRONG of rowdy bandits on the deck of the unfinished skyship jostle Sebastian as he moves through them. It's not out of any malicious intent. They don't register his presence any more than they do that of anyone else in the crowd. Because, again, his disguise is impeccable, *Meza*.

He makes his way forward without rushing. He doesn't want to look too conspicuous as he gets into position, so he throws himself around to the music. And now Sebastian can officially cross "moshing with bandits" off his bucket list, though he'd also need to add it first.

There's a new singer on the stage. This one's much better than the last one. Sebastian wouldn't suggest she quit her day job anytime soon, but she at least had the good sense to choose a song that hypes the crowd.

The singer isn't missing a beat of this chaotic "System of a Down" song. She chants nearly indecipherable lyrics then intones about going to the party and dancing in the desert before screaming about wars.

He's made it to his position at the side of Ruthless McTaggart's raised platform and can see the stage much better. And whoa! Is that real live piano music? Being played on a real live piano? By a real live piano player?

The stage is large, and on the right-hand side, a willowy man sits at the piano with his back to the audience. He bangs those keys like his life depends on it, his fingers moving like lightning.

The new plan is officially in motion. For now, there's nothing left for Sebastian to do but wait for Meza to complete her part. He might as well enjoy the show in the meanwhile. If this is how bandits get down, Sebastian might've had them pegged all wrong. Nobody who appreciates music this much can be all that bad.

The song comes to an end. Sebastian roars his approval along with the rest of the audience. There are some boos, but as the wise Jane Austen so aptly put it: It is a truth universally acknowledged that haters gonna hate.

Or something like that.

A man Sebastian had noticed on stage after the last performance strides out from the wings and takes the mic from the woman. He's in dark leather, complete with studs and spikes, with black smudged around his eyes.

He also wears a red bow tie.

Either this guy must be trying to single-handedly start a nerdcore fashion trend amongst the marauders, or this gathering of enemy crews must, indeed, be a special occasion.

"Give it up for Evil Eve, people!" the man shouts at the crowd. The crowd, accordingly, crank up their enthusiastic shouting. "And you know what? With a performance like that, I reckon she's going somewhere. *Eve*-entually."

And then he winks—actually winks—to make it clear that the travesty of a line was supposed to be a joke.

The cheering of the crowd flattens into boos. Sebastian winces. If he ever told a joke that corny, he'd immediately end his broadcast career.

The man plays off his bomb with a forced laugh. "All right. All right. Let's bring it down now so we can hear what our judges got to say."

Judges?

"What is going on here?" Sebastian mutters to himself, not for the first time.

On the left side of the wide stage, three bandits sit at a table, each with a mic propped before them. Sebastian wonders about those tabletop and—in the case of the performers on the stage—handheld mics.

They aren't strictly necessary for projecting a person's voice. The tiny built-in mic in his data cuff would get the job done as well as if not better than those. It must come down to style more than function. The bandits' mics are the type entertainers of old used way back before the age of the smart cities. Or at least modeled after them.

All at once, everything about this setup is outrageously familiar. The lone singer belting out popular hits. The audience, at times adoring but just as easily scornful. The smarmy host working the crowd. And of course, the panel of judges at the end of their careers and desperate for one last boost back into the good life.

It was only a few months ago that Sebastian broadcast the audio for Old World singing competitions on his radio show for two weeks straight, with his colorful commentary to help paint the picture. Some of those reality shows were painful to sit through, and yet he couldn't stop watching. Now the bandits are doing their own version.

This might be the best thing he's ever witnessed.

Is it too late to tell Meza to hold off on the plan until the show is over? He really does have to rethink his entire opinion about bandits. Turns out they really might be pretty cool.

The timbre of the audience lowers to a notch right below deafening as everyone's attention shifts to the judges.

The first judge at the table is unsmiling but grunts out a "Good. Very good."

The second judge sits forward and applauds. "Ain't never had so much fun in my life!"

The third judge leans back and tilts his head. "Look, Evil Eve, I respect you too much to lie. Your performance was a little…" He searches for the word. The audience quiets to a hush. "Pitchy."

Evil Eve's eyes bulge with rage. She launches herself across the stage before the judge has gotten out the second syllable of the word. In just a few large strides, she's at the table and then flying over it. She crashes into the judge, slamming him to the floor. The other judges jump back. The table topples.

The audience roars even louder than they had after her performance. This time, there is no booing.

"I'll show you pitchy!" she screams.

Sebastian can't exactly see what she's doing. The fallen table blocks his view. But there's blood. Lots of it.

The man standing center stage, the host, chuckles. "Looks like we'll need another judge."

The audience explodes with laughter.

Sebastian takes back his too-generous thoughts about these bandits maybe being okay. They are violent and crazy, and it's the worst combination to find in any group of people, let alone a group as fond of weapons as this one.

Evil Eve stands. Grinning, she licks a bloody finger.

Sebastian shakes his head. "So unhygienic."

But the crowd loves it, proving so by catching her after she leaps off the stage. They carry her on a wave of outstretched hands before swallowing her.

"Thank you, Evil Eve, for a right unforgettable performance," the host says. "And her song wasn't half bad either." He pauses here to lean toward the audience and give them a big, obvious wink. Then, to make sure they get that he's a fun guy, he adds, "I'm joking. I'm joking. You know I like to kid. It's my whole thing, right?"

Sebastian groans. Who gave this guy a mic? He's so bad Sebastian temporarily forgets the casual butchery he's just witnessed. Every time the host opens his mouth, Sebastian can practically see the energy draining from the audience.

"Okay," the host says, seeming to sense his own awkwardness, "let's bring up our next contender, Shitkicker!"

A new performer takes to the stage as a pair of bandits drag the body of the fallen judge into the wings. The table is righted and the judges take their place, including a new one to complete a new trifecta. At the cue, the piano player starts the next song.

And thus, it's on with the show.

So maybe this isn't exactly like the Old World singing competitions Sebastian is familiar with. They certainly wouldn't make an inspiring animated family film about this. Let alone a sequel.

If this is how they respond to mild criticism, he and Meza really need to not get caught. Sebastian glances upward, to where the distraction he's waiting for will appear at any moment.

The piano strikes up the chords of the next song. The singer has barely begun the first verse when a booming cacophony of 1980s synth overpowers all other noise in the cavernous building. Sebastian catches a flash of color and light from the corner of his eye. Everyone's attention leaps toward the source of the disruption.

This is it!

Sebastian moves without giving it a second thought. Stepping to the back of Ruthless's platform, he finds footing on the scaffolding and stealthily launches himself upward. Crouched on the edge of the platform, he's so close to Ruthless's huge chair he could reach out and touch it, but he should be in her blind spot, and the distraction is pulling her eyes away from him.

As the recorded Old World pop icon raps in German about a classical composer, Sebastian reaches out, almost casually, for the item on the little table beside Ruthless.

A glint of metal is his only warning.

Sebastian snatches his hand back only seconds before the vicious blade wedges into the table with a heart-lurching *thud*. That definitely would have stabbed right through the back of his hand.

His eyes travel from the knife that would have ended any ambition of making it as a hand model, to the fist gripping the knife's handle, up the scarred and muscular arm, and at last land on a sun-reddened face half covered in angry pink burn marks.

"Whaaaa?" Sebastian says in an impression of stunned confusion. "That ain't where I left my *Xanadu* DVD."

Ruthless McTaggert is not amused.

Sebastian finally notices that the distraction, the thing that was supposed to prevent this very situation, is incomplete.

Here's what should have happened.

At the same time that the music started up, there was to be the larger-than-life projection of Falco and his entire court from the *Rock Me, Amadeus* video. Except everyone in the projection would have had dancing T. rex bodies. Also, there would have been fireworks exploding in emojis.

After Sebastian told her the plan, Meza had asked, "Why don't you project a bunch of hellions or something?"

Sebastian looked at her, incredulous. "You think I got something like that programmed and ready to go at a moment's notice? What kind of a weirdo do you take me for?"

But back to the twenty-foot-tall projection of a classical-music-loving German rapper. The data cuffs that Meza was to plant at four different elevated points around the deck would have projected the baffling scene high, high above everyone's heads. It would have pulled every eye upward long enough for Sebastian to grab what they came for and slip away from Ruthless's platform before anyone noticed.

Instead, what he's seeing is a giant, lopsided Falco half emerged in the crowd of bandits. It looks like his big cotton-candy-topped head is rising up from the crowd like the sun on the eastern horizon. A few poop emojis float around the huge dome.

It pulled Ruthless's attention in exactly the worst direction. Right toward her side table and Sebastian, who has no good excuse for being there.

Meza never would have messed this up.

Scott Buddy.

Sebastian is sure that whatever went wrong, it's monster boy's fault.

Ruthless stands. She is a tall, tall woman and solidly built. This close, he notices her eyes are a surprising shade of hazel. On someone else, they would be stunning. On her, they're cold and menacing.

Sebastian scrambles to his feet, and only feels slightly less dwarfed by her. With their movement, the other bandits on the platform notice what's happening and rise too.

They close ranks around him. Many of their weapons look like they've been cobbled together from odds and ends they found lying around. Like they were made during bandit arts and crafts day. That doesn't make it any less unpleasant for Sebastian to find himself facing off against them.

His hands shoot up above his head. Standing inches from

the edge of the platform, Sebastian is all too aware of the lack of footing behind him.

"Easy, easy," Sebastian says. "Easy peasy."

"Stop the music." Ruthless's hard tone leaves no room for refusal.

"C'mon," Sebastian says. "What kind of monster cuts off Falco? This is the kinda song you gotta let play out." He bobs his head and shoulders to the beat, demonstrating how one properly responds to the iconic song.

"You reckon this is a time for jokes?"

"Not at all. But that ain't never stopped me before. Sometimes, I suspect I may have an unhealthy compulsion."

A small man with yellow teeth jumps in Sebastian's face. A sharp metal point presses into Sebastian's throat. "No one talks back to Ruthless, and no one makes her repeat herself. You gonna stop that music or regret being born?"

"Ha. I'll have you know I already beat you to that second one," Sebastian says, but he flicks his wrist to activate the holo-interface of his data cuff. He slowly stretches his arms above the small man's head, navigates to the program, and shuts it off.

This crowd of bandits doesn't have a concept of stillness or quiet, but in the absence of the upbeat music and colorful projection, their noise lowers to a dull rumble as more and more people catch on to the fact that something's happening on Ruthless's platform.

The small man backs off but takes Sebastian's blasters with him. Ruthless scrutinizes Sebastian from head to toe. Her frown deepens.

"You don't belong here," she says.

Impeccable as his bandit disguise may be, there's no making up for his lack of a tattoo marking him as a member of one of the crews. His commitment to a bit only stretches so far. He'd hoped he would blend in so well that no one would think to check his ink. Because what non-crewed-up idiot would willingly step foot into a bandit stronghold?

"I mean," Sebastian says, "who really belongs anywhere? Ain't life's journey about searching for that place only to discover it was inside of us all along?"

Ruthless stares at him for a moment that stretches on and on. Sebastian does his best not to crumble under her scrutiny. It's almost as if being on the receiving end of so many of Meza's glares has trained him for this very moment.

"An outsider has the nerve to think he can steal from me," she finally says.

"Would it make it better if I were a bandit?" This time, he isn't being smart. He's genuinely curious.

Sebastian can practically see news of his misdeeds spread through the audience as the bandits nearest the platform send her words to those farther back, to those who can't hear their conversation.

At last, Ruthless cracks a smile, and Sebastian doesn't like the sight of it at all. It's a small, cruel thing promising nothing good.

Quick as a whip, she snatches up the weapon resting against her chair, a tall and well-worn poleax. The blade end splits into all manner of pointy and stabby. Straight and sharp. Curved and sharp. Broad and sharp. So many ways to do irreversible damage to whoever's on the wrong side of that thing.

And right now, "whoever" happens to be Sebastian.

"Wait!" he cries as those pointy and stabby bits swing toward him.

"Take him to the stage." At the very last moment, Ruthless spins the weapon so that the blunted end comes at him.

He jumps back, avoiding the worst of the blow. But the result is the same. He flies backward and into the waiting crowd of unruly bandits.

6

ROUGH HANDS GRAB AT HIM. A jumbled blur of sneering faces leer at him. Taunts and laughter ring in his ears. He chokes on rank, alcohol-drenched breath.

The riotous wave carries him away from Ruthless's platform. They push him to the stage. Sebastian gladly clambers out of the rough hands. On steady ground again, he looks out over the audience and shivers.

"Thank you so very much for turning my dream of crowd-surfing into a nightmare," he tells the bandits nearest the stage.

The stage is even larger than it looked from the audience, but it is dwarfed by the building itself. From this new view, the scale of the shipyard blows his mind all over again. The unruly bandits clog the vast deck and fill every level of the ship's impossibly high cross-section. Staring up at the very top for too long could give a guy vertigo.

But instead of sending Sebastian into a panic, it gives him an odd sense of calm. This is an audience, after all. If there's one thing on this cruel Earth that he knows how to do, it's charm an audience.

Which is why he puts on a big grin, blows kisses, and raises his arms high over his head as if every single one of these filthy reprobates is screaming out a welcome and not for a bloody and entertaining end to his life.

The bow-tied host is crouched at the edge of the stage, consulting with the small man who'd held a knife to Sebastian's throat. The host glances toward Ruthless and nods before standing and addressing the crowd.

"Looky who we caught trying to steal our prize!"

The audience shouts threats and makes all manner of uncivil gestures.

Sebastian dips into a few gracious curtseys, pinched fingers holding out a pretend skirt at each side. The crowd roars even louder. It's yet to be determined whether his antics are amusing or further enraging them, but he's certainly giving them a show.

If he can get his hands on that mic, he might even stand a chance of talking his way out of this.

Bow Tie throws confused, sideways glances at Sebastian. This is probably the point at which someone else paraded before an audience of merciless bandits for the last moments of their life would cower and plead for leniency.

"This guy," Bow Tie says. "Trying to steal from us. Who does he think he is? *Steal*-y Dan?" Here, the host pauses for a laugh that doesn't come. "Oh, c'mon, guys! That was a good one! 'Cuz it's an Old World band. And we're doing music. But you gotta—you gotta imagine how it's spelled, right?"

The audience fidgets. Someone sends a chunk of debris skittering across the stage.

Sebastian cringes. Never explain obscure pop references, even if nobody gets them. Total rookie move. Unless this very awkward, eye-glazing scenario is what the host had been going for, but Sebastian doubts it.

The secondhand embarrassment is too unbearable.

Sebastian nudges the host and makes the universal gesture for "Move it along." Even though, yes, that means he's ushering things closer to his own public execution.

But how is he supposed to just stand there and let this slow torture drag on? He's not a sociopath.

"I got a fun surprise for you," Bow Tie says. "You'll like that, right?" What he likely meant to be a teasing tone comes out more like pleading. "I have been informed that since this here's a special occasion, our hostess has decided to let our special-guest bosses decide how we execute this fool."

Fool? That was a bit harsh. And here Sebastian thought he and Bow Tie were starting to become friends.

"But first," Bow Tie says, "Ruthless don't believe nobody's dumb enough to come in here and try this idiocy alone. And I reckon she's right."

"Oh, I'm quite the bonehead. Trust me," Sebastian says. "Some might even call it a gift."

"Whoever else don't belong might as well get on up here."

Predictably, neither Meza nor Scott Buddy reveal themselves. Meza understands that her remaining undiscovered gives them their best chance of leaving here alive.

"We're gonna find you," Bow Tie says over the audience. "It's only a matter of if you die together or all alone. Let's see which you prefer." Bow Tie pulls out a blaster and aims it squarely at Sebastian's chest. "You got three… two…"

"Hey," Sebastian interjects. "That ain't enough time for—"

"One." Bow Tie's finger twitches over the trigger.

And then Meza's there, pushing the blaster's nozzle upward. The sizzling shot flies toward the ceiling, harmless. But she isn't done. A fist to his nose and a twist of his wrist later, she's holding Bow Tie's blaster.

The audience goes wild.

A handful of Black Raven thugs, perhaps trying to show

their usefulness to their boss, charge the stage, various weapons drawn.

Sebastian zeroes in on the only weapon left at his disposal. He snatches the mic from Bow Tie, who is distracted by the fun sensation of having recently had his nose squished into his skull.

"Whoa, whoa, whoa!" Sebastian says into the mic. "Slow your roll. You can't blame her for having my back. Besides, you can't kill us. The honor of choosing the means of our demise goes to your illustrious bosses, remember? But she will gladly hand over the blaster."

Meza glares at the hulking figures surrounding her, but she knows, same as Sebastian, that this isn't going to be their big escape moment. She lets one of the thugs take the weapon.

"My nose!" Bow Tie cups his palms over his bloody face.

"Ouch," Sebastian says. "She got you good, didn't she? You ain't got nobody to blame but yourself. We all know the first rule of blaster safety. 'Watch where you point that thing, idiot!'"

That earns a scattering of chuckles from the crowd. It's a phrase every young Midlander hears when first learning to handle the weapons.

"I'll kill you!" Bow Tie shouts. Sebastian tilts the mic toward the host so that threats ring out. "I'll kill you both."

Sebastian raises an eyebrow at the audience. "Get in line."

The bandits respond with surprised but boisterous laughter.

"How'd you get up here so fast?" he asks Meza, lowering the mic.

"Already behind that curtain." She nods toward the wings.

"And Scott Buddy?"

"Lying low."

"I guess we'll see how that works out."

Bow Tie recovers his blaster and tucks it into its holster, and then he snatches the mic back with a growled "Gimme that!" Sebastian lets it go. For now.

"How're we getting rid of these pricks?" Bow Tie snarls. His words are slightly muffled by the reddening rag he presses to his nose.

"I think somebody's a tad bit upset that we upstaged him," Sebastian says to Meza then adds, "I'm gonna get us out of here. My brilliant plan's already in motion."

"What plan?" she asks.

"It's called charm and charisma."

"We're dead."

"Got any ideas, Oso?" Bow Tie turns to the platform on Ruthless's left.

The cushy setup not ten feet from the stage is similar to, if a bit smaller than, Ruthless's. A plump couch and a few armchairs are clustered around a low table cluttered with drinks.

The entourage occupying the extra seating carry themselves with that smug air of those who know they're exactly where everyone else wishes they could be, in the orbit of the actual very important person in their midst.

And *orbit* is exactly the right word in the case of the boss over the second-biggest crew in the Midlands.

They say that the Wild Raiders' El Oso Loco is as big as a bear, and real life doesn't disappoint. He takes up half of the couch all by himself and spreads out so he occupies far more than necessary. The other guy on the couch is forced to make do with whatever space is left, but then again, close proximity seems to be the idea there.

But Sebastian wouldn't call El Oso Loco rotund. The man just happens to be twice as wide and several heads taller than any other man on earth. His bushy beard and unruly hair make him look even more mountainous.

"Well, Bloody Bob…" El Oso's voice has the timbre of a man who gargles rocks every morning. Sebastian chuckles at the host's name. How perfect. Meza has already proven that the man does indeed bleed very well.

After a dramatic pause, El Oso shouts, "I say we tear him limb from limb from limb!"

The audience roars their approval. But Sebastian nearly yawns. How predictable. The guy who feeds people to his pet hellions wants to see him torn limb from limb.

Sebastian leans toward Meza. "Is it me, or for a minute there, did you think he was gonna say, 'Give them a good talking to and send them to bed without supper'?"

"Was on the tip of his tongue," Meza deadpans.

If the boisterous, hairy man is El Oso Loco, that means Blade and his inner circle must be in the VIP section on Ruthless's right. Except there's no bald man covered in head-to-toe tattoos, the description Sebastian has heard for The Basher's head honcho.

Instead, a young woman sits serenely in the center of the entourage.

She stands out among the rough-and-tumble crowd like a breeze of fresh air that's found its way over a trash heap.

Her dark hair is sculpted into perfect coils and tied back with a pristine white ribbon. Her mahogany skin glows against the yellow of a dress with more flounces and ruffles than should exist in this drab, utilitarian world.

And because in this messed-up world, even the soft things have sharp edges, she's dripping with blades. More axes than should be physically possible hang from straps that crisscross her torso.

Even with all that weaponry, Sebastian has never seen anyone look so… feminine. Unapologetically so.

She's cute.

Real cute.

And she's smiling at Sebastian.

Her finger curls a greeting that can only be interpreted as flirty.

Welp, Sebastian definitely isn't ready to die. Not when he's fallen in love for the first time in his life.

"No," Meza says to Sebastian.

"What?" He yelps like he's been caught sneaking dessert before dinner.

"Ain't what we're here for."

"I know that. I mean, my mind didn't even go there. And anyway, ain't you never heard of multitasking?"

"Aah," Bloody Bob—whose name Sebastian has already mentally amended to Bow Tie Bob—coos to the girl in yellow, "the lovely Sweetie Skull Crusher. What should we do with these two?"

Sweetie Skull Crusher leans over and whispers something to the young man sitting to her right. His ensemble is as out of place as hers, all clean lines and pastel colors that pop against his cool brown skin. Like something people might wear over in the Feudlands but not up here. Two enormous axes stick out from behind his back.

Meza levels a severe look at Sebastian. "Do something stupid, and I'll leave you to deal with the consequences yourself."

Sebastian snorts and gives her a disbelieving side-eye.

Now it's her turn to ask, "What?"

"You wouldn't leave little ol' me behind."

"Try me."

And of course Sebastian doesn't reply that some girls are worth dealing with a few pesky consequences. Not out loud anyway. Besides, Meza's the furthest thing from a romantic that a person can get. She doesn't understand matters of the heart.

Although she's right. Carousing with an intriguing young

woman is not what he came here for. Even if she is the most beautiful girl he's ever laid eyes on, and possibly the love of his life. And despite what he'd told Meza before they entered this place, he is quite capable of setting aside his own burning needs when the situation calls for it.

Expressionless, the dapper young man straightens and announces toward the stage, "Sweetie suggests you give the intruder to her. She'll make him suffer."

Sebastian nearly tackles Bow Tie Bob to get his hands on the mic. "Deal! I take that one! Let's do that one! Please, let's do that one."

Taken off guard, Bow Tie Bob's off-balanced attempt to wrestle the mic back fails.

Sebastian hops backwards and away from him as he speaks into the mic. "Is this guy really a bandit? I sincerely hope he's better at stealing stuff than he is at keeping it."

The crowd eats it up.

Sebastian throws a quick, assessing glance at Ruthless. Her hands are steepled before her face. She isn't laughing, but she also isn't calling for his or Meza's immediate execution. He considers that an encouraging sign. Even bandit queens appreciate good entertainment, right?

Bow Tie Bob whips out his blaster and takes aim, but Meza snatches it from him just as easily as she had before. This time, however, she tosses it to the back of the stage, where it disappears into the folds of black fabric.

"Wow," Sebastian says. "I was joking, but you really are epically bad at keeping stuff. Look, man, I think I got this. How's about you take a breather? See to that there nose."

He waltzes away from Bow Tie Bob and to the front of the stage without giving the host a chance to respond.

"What is up, Desperado City?" he shouts to the audience then holds the mic outward, encouraging their response.

They hoot and holler, enthusiasm pumped up to its highest setting.

"No, seriously," Sebastian says, making a show of taking in the stage. "What is happening here? This ain't what I expected when I decided to pay you all a visit. Who woulda guessed that this is how bandits spend their downtime?

"But I suppose y'all can't be all murder and mayhem all the time. Y'all deserve this, don't you? Banditry is hard freakin' work, ain't it? You know what? Have you given it up for yourselves today? Let's hear it for bandits!"

He points the mic toward the crowd again. They respond with an enthusiastic cacophony of cheers and whistles.

He shoots Meza a look, eyebrow raised. *Charm. And. Charisma.*

She raises an eyebrow right back. *Ain't running free yet.*

Bow Tie Bob looks between Sebastian and the crowd as if confused about how he so quickly lost control of the stage to this show stealer.

Charm.

And.

Charisma.

It's literally unfair that Sebastian doesn't come with a warning label.

"Can I say that it is truly a pleasure to be in the company of fellow music lovers? Being that you are all such appreciators of the melodic arts," he continues, "I got a solid hunch that you wouldn't want harm to befall me or my friend here."

"Just who the hell are you supposed to be?" El Oso bellows.

"How kind of you to ask, Mr. Loco. I'm none other than—"

"Sebastian Yun."

Sweetie's voice is louder and clearer than he'd expected. She might like pretty ribbons and soft dresses, but this is a woman who knows how to take command. "I'd recognize that voice anywhere."

A murmur ripples through the audience, his name carried from the crowd closest to the Basher's VIP section to those farther back.

It's as he's always telling Meza—never underestimate the power of celebrity.

"So you all've heard of the guy who hosts the only radio show in the world? Imagine that." After learning recently that sludgebrains had been tuning in to his broadcast, he will never again be shocked by anyone in his fan base. "If you give me a chance, I'd love to get to know some of you a little better."

This last part, of course, he directs at Sweetie. Her lovely grin doesn't falter. Her eyes invite him to make good on his proposition.

"And why is Sebastian Yun trying to steal from me?" Ruthless's voice is as even and stern as her expression. "And of all things, why this arm?"

She extends her hand. Like magic, the prosthetic arm in question lands in her palm, placed there by a member of her inner circle. And it's a thing of beauty. Not a crude piece of augmentation you can find anywhere. This is no chunk of wood with a hook shoved into one end of it. Even with all the Old World tech that has been scavenged and put to use across the Midlands, there's not much out there that compares to this piece of tech.

This arm is sleek. Every detail—the cool blue color, the elegance of the fingers, the perfectly articulated joints— speaks to an era when they had perfected cybernetic engineering and craftsmanship. The fact that it's still usable today, generations after it was first assembled, speaks volumes.

"Her name is Betty," Sebastian says.

Ruthless's eyebrow twitches. "Who?"

"The arm."

"The arm…"

"Betty. The Cybernetic Arm."

"Why is the arm's name Betty?"

"I mean… she definitely ain't a Cheryl."

"None of this explains why you're here. Stealing from me."

"Well, that's a funny story." Sebastian saunters across the stage and runs an appreciative hand across the smooth wood of the tall piano. "Almost as interesting, I'm sure, as how this beauty got here." His eyes land on the bespectacled middle-aged man at the keys. "You look to me like someone from the cultured regions of the Feudlands. You sneak in here too? I hear all the cool kids are doing it these days."

The man trembles. He doesn't dare look up from the black-and-white pattern beneath his fingers, as if his entire survival hinges on him making no eye contact whatsoever with anyone here. His clothes, though now very much the worse for wear, had once been nice. A hundred times nicer than anything anyone in the Midlands owns.

And there's a softness to him that's as out of place as his clothes, like he's gone his whole life without having to kill any monsters himself.

No wonder bandits put more energy into raiding and harassing their southernly neighbors. Sebastian supposes the Black Ravens stole the man at the same time they stole the piano. A matched set.

"Please!" the man whispers. "You have to help me! I have a family."

"Ain't you lucky," Sebastian whispers back, but then says into the mic, "Tell me something. Is it true that down south, them warlords of yours got whole wings of their citadels filled to the brim with countless wives? That the girls they chose ain't got no say in the matter any more than the boys got any say in 'volunteering' for their armies?"

"It's a great honor to serve our lord," the man mutters automatically. It's as if he's said those exact words so many times that he can't help himself, "with whatever talents we have to offer."

Sebastian swings back toward the audience. "That sounds like a yes to me. We may be miserable in the Midlands, but at least we got freedom to do whatever the hell we want."

The crowd roars. Bandits, apparently, are fans of freedom. Theirs, at least. They seem less concerned about that of the poor piano man—or of Meza and Sebastian's, for that matter.

No point in mentioning the fact that Feudlanders don't exactly let Midlanders hop and skip into their territories all willy-nilly.

"Although maybe not every bandit gets to enjoy their freedom equally." Sebastian wanders toward the three nervous-looking judges on the opposite side of the stage.

They must be bandits, if their black leather is any indication. A tattoo peeks out from under a woman's sleeve. The bottom half of the Black Raven's mark. Another judge has a Wild Raider mark inked on his neck.

"You don't seem especially happy to find yourselves on display up here." Sebastian's eyes drop to the still-wet blood staining the stage beneath the table. "Someone with a keener sense of observation might even venture to say you're expendable."

The Black Raven woman doesn't look particularly bothered by this truth. She nods. "Ain't nobody's fault but our own."

The Wild Raider man's spine straightens. He looks toward El Oso when he speaks loud and clear, his voice carried by the mic propped up on the table before him. "We done messed up. We're gonna earn our places back."

The crowd boos and jeers and throws trash at the stage. The judges take it in silence.

Sebastian strides back across the stage, clear of the flying detritus. "I gotta say, I love a good old-fashioned singing competition."

He glances toward Ruthless. It's hard to tell whether or not she's losing patience with him, but she makes no move to stop him. He takes that as explicit permission to continue full steam ahead.

"I know, I know," Sebastian says. "I ain't answered your question yet. But that's only 'cuz I got a better question. How do I intend to make it up to you? I can't help but notice that you're missing something. And it's a pretty crucial element of the talent competition format."

"Yeah?" El Oso shouts. "And what's that?"

Sebastian spreads his free arm out, offering himself up. "A celebrity judge."

The crowd approves. Loudly.

"Let me get this straight," Ruthless says. "After attempting to steal this contest's grand prize, you got the nerve to tell me that you should have a say in who goes home with it?"

"Anybody ever tell you that you got a gift for summation?"

She doesn't smile at his joke, and her ensuing silence stretches on for an agonizing eternity. Sebastian forces himself to keep his mouth shut.

He's played this game before. Usually, he's facing off against Meza. First one to speak loses. But unlike all those times when his need to spew clever quips and witty one-liners has doomed him, he can't let his tongue get the better of him now.

So he stands there looking cool, an easy grin on his face as if he has all the time in the world.

"C'mon, now," Sweetie Skull Crusher's voice rings out. "Let him do it. I reckon we'll have a good ol' time with him."

The hum of the audience lowers to a hush as Ruthless allows the question to hang in the air a few moments longer.

"I'll allow it," she says at last.

To the roar of the crowd, Sebastian bows, tosses the mic to the bewildered MC, and marches toward the judge's table.

Meza stops him with a hand on his shoulder. "Them judges' seats ain't an honor. It's a punishment."

"That fact did not fail to capture my notice."

"That smart mouth of yours ain't always the asset you think it is."

"Are you suggesting," Sebastian says, "that some of these artistes performing today may be a tad bit sensitive about receiving negative feedback and I better choose my words as if my life depends on it?"

"'Bout sums it up."

"I'll be on my very best behavior. But I ain't forgot why I'm here, and I ain't leaving without that arm."

7

SEBASTIAN IS TELLING a story that goes way back.

Back to before sneaking into the bandit stronghold. Before Scott Buddy's promise. Before those blue flags on the horizon.

Before, even, the fateful day that Sebastian and Meza met. Before he'd ever laid eyes on the broken-down hunk of metal that would become Her Royal Majesty.

"When I was fourteen," he says, "I got it into my thick head to go and take a stroll through one of them Intelli-Cities of old. All by my lonesome. Young me wasn't fixing to stick to the edge of the city, neither. I wanted to go deeper than even the most intrepid scavengers dare go. I wanted to see the heart of the place.

"Who knows why I decided I had to do it, but once my sight was set on it, nobody woulda been able to talk me out of it. If I had told anybody my plan, that is. Not like there was anybody I had to get permission from, or that I woulda asked even if there had been.

"That towering, sprawling city was something else. Another time. Another world. It was eerily quiet. Plants and trees had overrun everything, but all the structures were in incredible shape. Weirdly, it was all still orderly, but I suppose that was the AI at work before it was finally shut down.

"Then there were all the skeletons. Still there after all this time. That was the first time I really understood how many people never made it out of those paradises turned living nightmares and why, all these generations later, nobody wants to go back in.

"And look, I'm being one hundred percent real with you when I tell you that there were times when I woulda swore I heard human voices, whispers and sobbing. Laughter, once. But of course, when I looked over my shoulder, no one was there.

"Hell, I thought it had to be some sludgebrain laying a trap, and my dumb ass was gonna get eaten 'cuz what idiot goes that deep into a place like that all on his own? But no sirree. There was never nobody there, man nor monster, to explain them noises I heard. Them cities are all tombs better left untouched, I tell you what. Memorials of humanity's downfall.

"Now, I didn't know that I went in there looking for something. Not until after I was already standing in them ruins, and then I had no idea what I was supposed to be looking for. But I couldn't leave until I found it. And I would eventually find it. Knew it was what I came for the second my gaze fell upon it."

Sebastian's eyes land on Betty the Cybernetic Arm, back at its place on the table at Ruthless's side. The things he goes through for that arm.

The entire audience of bandits, the building itself, the very seconds seem to be holding their breath. He has transported them, and they hang on his every word.

He's never told this story before. Not on his show, not to

Meza. This tale requires him to come too close to memories that he avoids like he owes them a debt. But they've been there, at the edge of everything, from the moment he spotted those blue flags. It's no surprise this previously unspoken tale resurfaced.

"It wasn't easy to locate," Sebastian continues. "As a matter of fact, it was an accident that brought me to it. A man with grandiose ideas about his place in the universe would call it fate. So yeah, it was fate. After spending days in the company of ghosts and phantoms, I finally high-tailed it out of that Intelli-City and never looked back.

"That place was scary. But that doesn't compare..." He pauses here. The moment requires a little drama. "...to how scary good that performance was!"

He rises to his feet, giving the performer a one-man standing ovation. His fellow judge pops to her feet and joins in. Then the audience is cheering on the mohawked bandit with a falsetto made for covering Earth, Wind, and Fire.

Mohawk Guy's mouth is sculpted in a severe frown. Sebastian braces to duck beneath the judges' table.

Not even these insane people would take out a guy who gives them a rave review...

Is what Sebastian thought before four contestants ago.

Four contestants ago, one of the judges learned that there was such a thing as being too nice. Her strategy had obviously been that if she had nothing critical to say, no contestant could possibly have a reason to wish her harm.

And that strategy worked for seven rounds of judging.

Until one man made it abundantly clear that he had strong feelings about being patronized.

So anyway, three judges are now down to two—Sebastian and a woman with a large round nose ring hanging above her lips. When he'd first taken a seat at the table, there'd been four judges. Neither of the two fallen judges had been replaced. The bandits must have run out of their supply of volunteers.

Center stage, Mohawk Guy's frown splits open into a teeth-baring scowl. Sebastian swallows. Death by singing competition. At least it's a novel way to go.

A single manly tear slides down Mohawk Guy's left cheek.

"I will never forget this, Sebastian Yun." The deep gravel of Mohawk Guy's voice after those sky-high runs confuses Sebastian almost as much as the bandit's words. He still isn't quite sure whether this man plans to murder him or not. Until Mohawk Guy adds, with literally zero inflection, "I ain't usually this emotional. Your words done moved me. I am very happy."

Sebastian nods, suspecting that Mohawk Guy's scowl is actually maybe a smile—or as close to one as he can get. The man returns the nod and replaces the mic on its stand before leaving the stage.

Legs turned to rubber, Sebastian sinks into his seat. "Please tell me we're almost done."

Somehow, he's still alive, having managed to charm-and-charisma his way through the last twelve performances and dishing out feedback for singers both good:

"If facing the threat of public execution is what it takes for me to hear that golden voice again, I might have to come here and get caught stealing from Ruthless every day."

And bad:

"I ain't gonna lie. Is your voice a thing of beauty? We both know it ain't, right? That said, I really need to thank you for allowing me to witness that showmanship! You, madam, are a true entertainer. You owned that stage. I could watch you perform for hours. That is, if y'all don't kill me first. Heh, heh."

Sebastian raises an eyebrow at his one remaining cojudge, a woman who'd earlier introduced herself as "Arrow. Big fan."

"And you volunteered for this?" Sebastian asks her.

"You did, too, didn't you?" Arrow says, good-natured. Her nose ring shifts when she smiles wide. She can't be much older than Sebastian, maybe barely in her twenties. So far, she's taken this all in stride.

Having been at the judging table before Sebastian got there, Arrow is the longest-surviving judge yet. She might actually make it through this thing. She's proven herself to be smart enough to let Sebastian speak first during the judging. After Sebastian has disarmed everyone with a laugh, the contestants have proven themselves to be a lot less murdery.

On the stage, Bow Tie Bob the MC hams it up for the impatient audience while, across the stage, the next singer—a woman with half her head shaved—is having what looks like a heated conversation with the Feudlander at the piano. At least, her side is heated. The Feudlander nods quickly while keeping his head down.

This is the longest break between performances that the judges have gotten so far. Sebastian appreciates the breather.

"Well," he says, "it looked like things were leaning toward public execution for me. I figured this might let me get out of here with a pulse."

"Same here. Broke the rules and just hoping to see another day."

"Back up. Bandits got rules? Did y'all forget the part about being lawless scoundrels?"

"You know, I thought the same thing before I joined up with the Black Ravens. Ruthless takes her rules real serious. But once a year, she offers a way back into good standing. Calls it the Trial of Redemption. Judging this here contest ain't nothing compared to last year's trial."

"Which was?"

"Cage fights. Actually, it's been that every year before this one, or so I'm told."

"See! That's what I was expecting."

"Compared to that, this here's real cushy." Arrow leans back in her chair, hands folded behind her head. "Alls I gotta do is survive this, and I'm home free."

"You know, Arrow, I like you. Your vibe in the face of probable death is refreshing. I get tired of being the only chill dude in the room."

She shrugs. "Never expected to live long anyway. I'm riding this train as far as it'll take me. If this turns out to be my last stop, then I guess that's that. Getting bent out of shape before I get there ain't gonna do much to change that."

"Exactly!"

"No, no, no!" Bow Tie Bob is saying to the woman arguing with the Feudlander on the other side of the stage. A weapon has been pulled. "No stabbing the piano man, Stone-Eyed Songco. We still need him."

"Gotta say," Arrow tells Sebastian, "never seen the boss extend the Trial of Redemption to an outsider."

"The power of charm and charisma." Sebastian sends a smug glance toward Meza.

She sits with Ruthless's entourage. After Sebastian was made a judge, the question of what to do with Meza came up. She declined to volunteer as a judge. El Oso Loco had extended an invitation for Meza to sit with him. The offer came with a pat of his lap and a few other lewd gestures. This despite the handsome man already tucked under his arm.

Meza had wordlessly considered her options and then hopped off the stage and mounted the steps of Ruthless's platform. She took a seat near the feared ruler. Sebastian couldn't even be sure Meza realized she'd so casually claimed a coveted spot among the Bandit Queen's inner circle.

For her part, Ruthless cocked an eyebrow, but she

allowed it. Meza might not have charm and charisma, but she certainly has something working for her.

She doesn't catch the look Sebastian throws her way. She and Ruthless are exchanging words, neither of them smiling, neither of them saying more than a few words at a time. There's nothing hostile about the interaction, as near as he can tell. Both women simply aren't smilers. And extremely terse.

Sebastian blinks, experiencing something like… Is there a word for something like déjà vu but for something that hasn't happened yet? And when it happens, it will be somebody else's experience?

Despite the two of them looking nothing alike, watching them is like seeing Meza have a conversation with her future self. Does Ruthless see her seventeen-year-old self reflected in Meza's younger face?

"Well," Sebastian says, pulling himself back to his conversation with Arrow, "as you have observed, I am incredibly good at this. You can go on and relax now. I'll see us through to the end of this thing."

"This here's the easy part," Arrow says. "Wait until the bosses perform."

"The who does what now?"

She waves at the stage, where the latest performer is finally taking her place. "These guys, they know they ain't got no chance of winning. They're showing off, hoping to get their egos stroked. But mark my word, when the bosses get on that stage, each one of them will be expecting to walk away with that prize. And the losers will not be happy. And who do you reckon they'll take it out on?"

The notes of Miami Sound Machine swing and sway up from the piano.

"I really shoulda asked more questions before signing up for this," Sebastian says.

"The thing about them cage fights we usually do, they are always to the death. Only one person ever comes out of them alive. Sometimes, not even that. We ain't really expected to come through this with our lives. It's only a tiny sliver of hope that got us up here. Besides, what other choice do we got? Reckon we wouldn't make it far if we tried to run."

Her air of indifference falters. A far off look crosses her face, like she's doing the math in her head and doesn't like what it adds up to.

It's not news that taking the judge's seat might only provide a temporary stay of execution. Still, facing the wrath of two unhappy crew bosses would make things trickier than they already are.

On stage, the performer demands that everyone do the conga. The delivery is choppy, the performer's nerves getting the better of her, but the man on the piano is killing it.

How can Sebastian sink into despair when he feels the rhythm and it is indeed getting stronger? It's biologically impossible to worry about anything when this song is playing.

"Let's not be overdramatic," Sebastian says. "If it's a talent thing, there's gonna hafta be a clear winner. Unless you want me to believe that all three of them bosses got singing chops. I reckon that ain't what you bandits think of when you hear the term 'triple threat.'"

Arrow's lazy grin returns. "I hope you're right."

Sebastian is sure he is. He's gotten out of worse scrapes than tangling with singing and dancing bandits. As far as he's concerned, it isn't time to start panicking yet.

·····||·||||·|···||·||||·|·||·||·····

LATER.

Though not much later.

It's after Sebastian and Sweetie have gotten… close.

And incidentally, not long before she attempts to give him his much-needed haircut, scalp and all.

El Oso had demanded a break. Sebastian took the impromptu intermission as an opportunity to wander away for a bit, which may or may not have been long enough for him to get into even more trouble. But now it's time to return to his judge's seat.

With the front curtains pulled closed at El Oso's insistence, the stage is dim, which matches Sebastian's prospects for his immediate future.

He finds Meza posted at the judges' table, clearly waiting for him.

"You come to check on my well-being?" Sebastian says. "I'm touched."

"Seen Scott Buddy?" she asks.

"I'm good. Thanks for asking. Well, two out of the three bandit bosses in attendance done threatened me in the last ten minutes. So maybe slightly less than good?"

He reconsiders his earlier conversation with Arrow. He perhaps should have taken her warning to heart. He definitely shouldn't have given in to temptation and sauntered off during the break.

Meza gives him a flat look.

"I did literally nothing to exacerbate matters," he insists. "Well, maybe I kinda did. But that was only a teeny tiny part of it."

Sebastian thinks back to that moment before they entered Desperado City, when he realized that she supported what he was trying to do here. Because she thought he was taking his first steps toward becoming selfless or responsible or some nonsense like that.

It's little moments like this that teach her the important

lesson of not putting her faith in him. She'll learn eventually to stop expecting him to be anyone but who he is.

"Scott Buddy," Meza says, offering no reaction to his rambling confession.

"I saw it a little while ago. It was freaking out. I gave it a stirring inspirational speech and sent it on its way. It's probably still lurking around here. We might even get out of here without it giving itself away as a creature of evil. Assuming we get out of here."

"They ain't—"

"Yeah, yeah. What were you and Ruthless in deep conversation about earlier?"

"She tried to recruit me. Told me I ain't gotta start at the bottom. Got a place for me at her side. Said you don't deserve me."

"Rude."

Meza shrugs.

"You told her she was flat-out wrong, right?" Sebastian says. "That I, in my own unique way, contribute to this here partnership?"

"Want me to lie to the woman?"

Sebastian gasps and clutches at invisible pearls.

"There you are!" Bow Tie Bob materializes at Sebastian's side. He holds a stack of paper cut roughly into small rectangles. "I been trying to get a moment with you."

"You don't wanna do revenge on me for upstaging you earlier, do you? I'm way over today's quota for bandit threats."

"Not at all. If I'd known who you were from the beginning, I'da handled all that completely differently. You're my idol, Sebastian Yun!"

"Go on."

"I studied you and what you do on your show for a whole month to prepare for hosting this here event."

"Huh," Sebastian says. "So this was you making an effort."

"Well, I have always been a naturally funny person. My mama told me so every day. But being on stage in front of all them people, I gotta admit, it's harder than it looks. So I was thinking, I got these ideas for some jokes I could try out. I'm hoping you can flip through them and tell me which ones I should run with."

Bow Tie Bob thrusts his stack of paper at Sebastian.

"Oh. I'm super honored that you'd ask..." Sebastian pauses, trying to think of a nicer way to say that he'd rather slather himself in molasses and lie naked on top of a fire ant hill.

"I ain't got all day," El Oso thunders. "Get out there and introduce me, Bloody Bob!"

The big man has taken up position in the center of the stage, flanked by several of his underlings. They've changed into new clothes. New *coordinated* clothes. The wings of the stage are crowded with even more Wild Raiders.

Bow Tie Bob deflates and tucks his little papers into his pocket.

"We can go over these together later," he promises.

"Wait." Sebastian nods at the empty judges' table. "Where's Arrow?"

"Oh," Bow Tie Bob says. "She tried to run. Didn't get far. Guess she thought her odds were better trying to escape than to face the rest of the competition. Can't say she's wrong."

"I'm guessing she won't be returning to the judges' table."

"Hard for a corpse to judge anything."

"Bloody Bob!" El Oso bellows.

"I'm rooting for you, brother!" the host says, scurrying away from Sebastian. "Oh! And if you don't die today, I was thinking maybe I could come on your show sometime and try some of my material out on the air."

"Can you believe that?" Sebastian turns to Meza, but she's

already slipped away, probably in fear that Bow Tie Bob would attempt to try out some of his "material" on her.

Sebastian is utterly alone when he takes his place at the table. He's the last judge standing in a competition where two-thirds of the remaining contestants have made it clear that they're going home with the prize, and there will be hell to pay for the guy who tells them differently.

It might be time to start panicking.

8

"OH, CRAP!" Sebastian breathes, transfixed. "She's good. Really, really good."

It's minutes before the intermission and before Sebastian learns that he is the last judge standing.

He's listening to the clearest, purest sound he has ever heard. Sweetie's sultry voice is like a crystal.

She takes her time with the slow start to the Alicia Keys song, drawing out the notes so that each one is an experience unto itself. And she's doing all of this completely a cappella. A bold choice with this unruly audience who prefer fast-paced, raucous performances. But she grabs hold of every-one's attention and refuses to let go.

Her voice.

Her presence.

That's all Sweetie needs to command the stage.

He has no problem believing every lyric she pours into him as the absolute truth. Of course, she is on fire. Of course, she is hot. Of course, she can fly. And of course, 100 percent, she is burning it all down.

She lets go of a long, beautiful note then lets its impact

hang in the air as the heavenly sound floats away. She makes the audience wait for more. And they do, collective breath held.

The piano starts up. The music is not what Sebastian expected. It's something new, built on top of the original.

Sweetie's well-dressed right-hand man is at the keys. When he'd marched up to the stage and booted the Feudlander from the piano bench, Sebastian had watched in confusion.

No one in the Midlands knows how to play music. Who has time for it with all the day-to-day work of surviving? Plus, where would they get the instruments to practice on?

But the young man really knows how to play. Really, really knows how to play. Sebastian can't even fully marvel at the miracle that is a Midlander with the skills to work an instrument, let alone a piano, because Sweetie's performance overshadows everything.

She transforms the shipyard.

This isn't a dingy, rusting warehouse. Sweetie isn't standing on a rough-hewn stage with musty black curtains. Her audience isn't a horde of drunk, dirty bandits.

This is an arena with 360-degree seating, dazzling lights, and an ear-shattering sound system. She's a diva, filling stadiums, stealing hearts, and inspiring lifelong devotion. These are her fervent fans. They should have a collective moniker. Sweetie's Toothaches or something equally ridiculous.

After the second verse, the music changes as she climbs the hook. Sebastian has just recognized the new song that her man on the piano has artfully mashed up with the first when Sweetie smoothly switches from belting out about a girl on fire to taunting her audience about what bad bad girls do well.

She doesn't give the crowd much time to appreciate her

inspired take on the M.I.A. chorus before the music changes up again. A Whitney Houston song.

Without missing a beat, Sweetie declares that she is the queen of the night. Her subjects roar their support for her reign as she struts across the stage. Her aura inspires worship, and the audience gives it eagerly. She demands an offering. Obediently, hands lift to create a new beat on top of the piano chords.

Sebastian watches Sweetie, but he watches the audience as well, speechless. The electricity shared between this true entertainer and her audience is like nothing he's ever experienced. Never could have ever imagined.

The performance comes to an end too soon. And from the roar of the crowd, everyone agrees.

She's looking directly at Sebastian, waiting.

Why?

Sebastian blinks away his reverie. He's supposed to be saying something clever right now.

His brain is mush.

He clears his throat to buy himself time to remember how to do that talking thing. He's supposed to be good at that, right?

"Sweetie..." he manages.

"Sebastian," she replies.

Her gaze is steady. He couldn't look away from her if he wanted. They might as well have the entire shipyard to themselves.

It occurs to Sebastian that the answer to his problem of getting Betty back is simple.

Simple and maybe impossible.

And if it just so happens to mean he must spend a little one-on-one time with this mesmerizing songstress, then so be it.

"You," Sebastian says, "are the queen of the night, the day, the entire freakin' universe. I could watch you all day."

"Don't go falling for me, now," Sweetie says. "Wouldn't be fair to the other contestants."

"Might be a little late for that."

A rough, boisterous voice crashes into their private world.

"What's the difference between a dying cat and Sweetie's singing?" El Oso doesn't wait for any guesses. "When it's Sweetie's singing, you wanna put yourself out of your misery."

Sweetie moves before El Oso has finished his first guffaw. An ax glints through the air and, with a THWAK, embeds itself into a spot on the couch right between his knees. A few inches up and, well—if El Oso has any kids, hopefully, he likes them, because that would've been the end of his line.

"I'll gladly put you out of your misery, old man." Sweetie smiles cordially. "Say the word."

El Oso smirks back and then abruptly stands. "I demand a break. Unlike some ax-crazy brats I know, my performance won't put everyone to sleep. My crew needs time to prepare for the only real show you'll see today."

The curtains jerk closed, cutting everyone on the stage off from the audience. In the resulting dimness, Sweetie captures Sebastian's attention with a lingering look and mischievous grin then turns and disappears through the backdrop curtains. Sebastian snaps to his feet.

Invitation received.

Bow Tie Bob, who'd been in the wings, frantically scribbling on little sheets of paper, grabs the mic Sweetie had dropped to the stage and parts the curtains to let himself through to the audience.

"So, I—uh," the host says from the other side of the

curtains, "I got some new stuff to try out on you. Let's see." The sound of paper shuffling. "Oh, you'll like this one."

Tuning him out, Sebastian stretches his arms over his head oh-so-casually and yawns.

"Welp, this seems like a good time to go take a leak. So that's what I'll be doing. Yep. Just gonna go find the ol' water closet."

Pretending he doesn't hear Arrow call out, "Toilets are the other way," Sebastian slips behind the backdrop curtains, accepting Sweetie's wordless invitation.

···|||·|||||·|···|||||·|·|||···

IT'S SHORTLY after Sebastian and Sweetie have gotten... close, and moments before he learns that he's the last judge standing.

The intermission is almost over as Sebastian makes his way back to the stage.

Things did not go according to plan.

Far beyond the stage's backdrop, on the part of the deck Sebastian thinks of as the vehicle graveyard, the maze of hollowed-out trucks and partially rebuilt ATVs offered relative solitude and distance from the noise. By comparison, everything directly behind the backdrop is pure chaos.

Rough men and women brandishing the Wild Raiders' flaming skull tattoo dart around. Some haul equipment through the backdrop and up a short flight of steps to the stage. Several bandits pull on matching ensembles.

On his way up the backstage steps, Sebastian skirts a pair of men hauling a huge, clunky piece of equipment. As he parts the backdrop curtains, he collides with El Oso Loco.

The mountain of a man glares down at him.

"Sorry," Sebastian says, distracted. "I didn't expect nobody to park Mount Kilimanjaro at the top of these steps."

El Oso's scowl unfurls into a toothy grin. A knowing glint flashes in his eyes. "Well, well. If you ain't got the look of a man who bit off more than he can chew."

"I ain't quite sure what you mean," Sebastian says, though unfortunately, El Oso has summed his mood up pretty much perfectly.

Arms crossed, El Oso looks over his shoulder. "And they call me crazy. You must really like living on the edge, don't you?"

Sebastian follows his gaze to the other side of the dim stage. Sweetie and her well-dressed right-hand man share a quiet conversation. She doesn't spare a glance toward Sebastian.

What was it Sebastian had thought when he first saw her? In this messed-up world, even the soft things have sharp edges. He wishes he hadn't been proven right quite so quickly.

·····|||||||||·|·····|||||·|·|·||·····

IT'S mere moments before Sebastian collides with El Oso backstage.

Sebastian and Sweetie are… close. Her feminine form pressed against him is a surprise he more than welcomes.

He can't tell anybody else what to do when the hot girl they've been crushing on all day pushes them against the side of a truck and starts kissing them like she's trying to steal all the breath in their lungs. But to him, it only seems fair that he should do his damnedest to steal all her breath right back.

They're the only two in the sprawling vehicle graveyard. Dozens of vehicles in various states of repair and their gutted components create a labyrinth of rusted metal and filthy machine parts. The noise of carousing bandits feels so very far away.

"Wait… Wait!" Sebastian pulls his face away.

"What?" Sweetie says.

"I'm gonna ask for a favor later, and I don't want you thinking I seduced you to get it."

She laughs. "That's how this situation's playing out in that head of yours? You're the one doing the seducing?"

"Don't underestimate my wiles."

"Stop talking."

"Yes'm."

Lips meet. Hands explore. Hearts race.

"Wait… Wait!"

"What?" she says in an impatient breath.

This close, he notices the stunning hazel of her eyes, green speckled with iridescent gold.

"What about your boyfriend?" he asks. "I sorta promised someone I'd do better about avoiding unnecessary trouble. Pissing off a bandit for touching his girl would maybe break that promise."

"This someone aware that you tried to steal from a whole citadel full of bandits today?"

"But it was necessary."

"Even if I decided I wanted a boyfriend," she says, "what I do with myself wouldn't be up to him."

"So your dapper right-hand man…?"

"You mean Tom? Gross. He's my brother."

"Oh. *Ooooh—*"

She cuts him off with an attack on his lips, but he pulls away an instant later.

"His name's Tom? Not Sharp Fang or Murder Guy or Jagged Shard of Glass?"

"I'm done discussing my brother."

"Yes'm."

And for a while, Sebastian is perfectly content to forget about the powder keg waiting for him when the competition restarts. If there is a chance that this day ends tragically for him, doesn't he owe it to himself to enjoy the here and now? All of that can wait. Betty can wait.

Something gnaws at him.

He ignores it.

He *really* wants to ignore it.

It's like trying not to notice a gnat flitting in his face.

"Wait… Wait!" This time, it takes nothing less than Herculean effort for Sebastian to lean away from Sweetie. Well, to lean his face away. His hands and his body are decidedly more committed to keeping her close than his words would suggest.

"Seriously?" she says.

He groans, resists the urge to kiss that little frown off her full lips. "Apparently so. It's just—I'm sure we ain't got a lot of time—"

"Why do you think I skipped the wining-and-dining part?" She runs a finger down his exposed stomach. The light, teasing touch sends a shiver through his body. Whoever invented crop tops for dudes is a freakin' genius.

He catches her hand, folds it in his. He needs to focus. This is not what he came after Sweetie for.

Or at least, not the only thing.

"I really gotta ask you something. And you're likely to think I done lost my mind for even suggesting it—" Naturally, he doesn't get all of this out in one go. He keeps having to stop to kiss her here and kiss her there. Whether she's on stage or in his arms, there's something addictive about this girl.

"Spit it out, pretty boy," she says.

"Fairly sure you mean ruggedly handsome man."

"Yeah, of course." She doesn't sound entirely convincing, but Sebastian is willing to let it go. For some reason that he can't put his finger on, he's finding it really difficult in this moment to imagine ever being upset with her.

They're kissing again. That may have something to do with it.

She turns to stone against him. It's the type of tense stillness that signals danger.

"Wha—" Sebastian reaches for a blaster that isn't there. In the same instant, he pivots, following her startled gaze to the monster perched on the edge of the truck's roof.

···|||||||||·||··||||||||·||·|||···

"NO SIRREE," Sebastian says in response to El Oso's backstage question regarding a preference for living on the edge. "I'd actually prefer to live a safe, cushy way of life, but what can you do?"

The colossal man claps his enormous hand onto Sebastian's shoulder. Sebastian teeters. It's like holding up a stack of bricks. El Oso tightens his grip and drags him farther onto the dim stage, out of the way of the two Wild Raiders carting the big piece of equipment.

It's just one of several machines that were added to the stage while Sebastian was otherwise occupied.

"The risks you take with your life are up to you," El Oso says. "But I got expensive tastes. That arm will go a long way toward keeping me in the lifestyle to which I have become accustomed."

"I imagine it takes a lot to keep the belly of a guy like you satisfied."

El Oso's laugh nearly shakes the stage. "You're funny. I like you."

"Wow, thanks. Are we best friends now?"

"But if I happen to lose my prize because Sweetie curried favor with one of the judges…" He pulls Sebastian close.

Sebastian can practically taste whatever it was that crawled into the bandit's mouth and died. "I will not be happy. And that is a risk I'd advise you not to take."

SWEETIE DROPS TO THE GROUND, where her ax holsters had at some point ended up. Sebastian reaches toward his hip seconds before remembering that he's blasterless thanks to the bandits taking his weapons.

She frees one of her deadly weapons in a fluid motion, takes aim at the eerie figure perched on top of the truck they'd been leaned against.

Sebastian dives, catching her arm before she releases the throw.

"What the hell?" The jab from her free hand comes too fast for him to avoid. Wham, bam, right in the diaphragm, ma'am.

He falls back, clutching his abdomen.

"Know… i—him…" Sebastian wheezes as she raises her ax once again.

Though why he's bothering to save Scott Buddy may forever remain a mystery.

The monster in question continues to watch, unblinking, from the roof of the truck. "Sebastian Yun. We are talking later, yes? We are waiting."

Sweetie doesn't lower her ax. "This kid a friend of yours?"

Sebastian rolls his eyes but nods. Reluctantly.

"I thought…" She shakes her head. "I don't know what I thought."

Sebastian suspects that she thought she had looked up to find an apex predator looming over her, that her instincts had screamed *Fight! Fight! Fight!* for good reason.

She points toward Scott Buddy with her weapon. Her

smile is even more wicked than her blade. "But you wouldn't be the first peeping Tom to lose an eye to one of my axes."

Sebastian lifts his arms and folds his hands behind his head, sucking in air through his teeth. Sweetie really knows how to throw a punch.

The worst part of this situation is how the perfect quip about her taking his breath away is going to waste, what with him barely able to speak and all. Instead, he uses the precious resource of his words to get to the point.

"Go away, Scott Buddy."

"But—"

"Away. Go. You. Find Meza."

"Meza is talking to angry lady. Too many people. We are not wanting to stop Sebastian Yun and Sweetie Skull Crusher. Smashing faces again, yes? We are waiting. Very quiet. See?"

It waves a hand, giving them permission to continue what they'd been doing moments ago.

"Oh, we are so gonna have a talk about why that ain't okay," Sebastian says, relieved that his breathing and speaking have mostly returned to normal. He turns to Sweetie. "You mind if I take a second to get rid of iii—him?"

Again, he barely catches himself at the last minute. The last thing he needs right now is to have to explain to Sweetie why Scott Buddy is an "it."

"Fine." The word sits right on the cusp of this actually being fine and her being over him by the time he comes back.

Sebastian rounds to the other side of the truck. Scott Buddy nearly gives him a heart attack when it leaps down to meet him with inhuman grace and speed. He hopes Sweetie couldn't see too much from her vantage point.

"Which one are you?" Sebastian hisses. It's unlikely that Buddy's in control, not with the way the sludge has been acting lately. But Scott had been doing well with remembering to speak in the singular. Whichever of them had been speaking just now had been using "we."

"We are Scott."

"What do you want, Scott? Besides to ruin another plan."

"Many humans here. More than we are seeing… like this."

"You mean free? Not enslaved and trapped in their own bodies by a bunch of body-snatching slime creatures?"

Scott nods. "Bandits are not like Sebastian Yun and Meza. Not like humans in Hopeful camp. And we are not having Meza telling us what to do."

Scott hunches to the ground, traces mindless shapes in the dirt and grime with a finger.

"We are not knowing what to say," it says, "or how to act. Bandits are very much yelling and fighting and pushing and… and talking to us and Buddy is saying nothing always and this is being… this is being… too much."

"What exactly do you expect me to do about it?"

"Sebastian Yun is telling us how to be normal." Scott looks up with big, earnest eyes. But it casts its eyes down again when it adds, quietly, "How to be… human."

Sebastian glances around, like maybe Meza will decide to pop out of nowhere and deal with this for him. They don't officially have a chore roster, but it goes without saying that babysitting monster boy would fall squarely under her column.

He rubs the back of his neck and sighs. "Okay, look. First of all, ain't nobody like me. Matter of fact, same goes for Meza. But mostly me. Secondly, don't go putting too much stock in 'normal.' Ain't nothing normal about this world or the folks living in it.

"And lastly, this one's for Buddy." Sebastian leans in closer, peering through Scott Buddy's eyes as though he can catch a glimpse of the parasite if he looks hard enough.

"You better be listening in there, you puddle of goo. You

can't go raising a kid with *you* as the only thing he—it—talks to for ten years then just throw it out to the wolves and leave it to fend for itself. So—and I can't believe I'm saying this—come out and give the kid a break. Pull your weight around here."

Scott shakes its head. "No, no. We are knowing Buddy is sad. We are handling."

"Are you? Is that why you done reverted back to the royal 'we'? Whatever. You asked me a question, and I gave you an insightful and poignant answer. Now, if you don't mind, I got business to get back to, and you need to go away."

Sebastian returns to the side of the truck that offers significantly more desirable company.

Sweetie is absently twirling an ax, one hand on her hip, the very picture of danger and desire. But before he can be pulled back into the delicious distraction of her kisses and caresses, he blurts out his question.

"Assuming you win," he asks, "what would it take for me to convince you to give me that arm?"

····ıılı|ılı|ııılı||ııı|lı|ılı|ıı····

NOT THAT EL OSO'S threat isn't convincing, but his words might've had more of an impact if the whole "creepy threat two inches from Sebastian's face" thing hadn't already been done in very recent history.

So as it is, Sebastian only experiences a bit of my-heart-stopped-for-a-millisecond terror instead of oops-my-ghost-just-left-my-body terror.

He places his own hand on El Oso's shoulder, though it doesn't seem to quite have the same effect as when the big man had done it to him.

"I'ma go 'head and ask the obvious question," Sebastian

says. "If you want the coveted prize so bad, why not do what bandits do best and take it?"

"We got a code."

"Wow. And it covers singing competitions? That is extensive. If I ever need some legal documents drafted, I know where to come."

"We don't steal from each other."

"Oh, right, right, right. That makes more sense."

El Oso doesn't lower his arm, so neither does Sebastian, even though he's starting to feel a little ridiculous standing like this.

"So let me get this straight," Sebastian says. "Stealing from each other is a big no-no, but killing each other all willy-nilly and eating up smaller gangs, that's fair game?"

El Oso convulses with laughter, shaking Sebastian's lean frame along with him.

"Apparently, I've made a funny?" Sebastian says.

El Oso leans back and gives Sebastian a friendly punch to the shoulder. Sebastian stumbles but manages to remain upright. The bruise is probably already forming.

"You think we assembled here just to sing and get drunk?" El Oso says.

"I mean, y'all are singing and drinking, so...'

"This here's the after party, friend. Me, Ruthless, and Sweetie done spent the morning negotiating territories, distributing disability payments, and hearing petitions from smaller crews that want to merge with us. And afterward, we celebrate. Same as us bosses do every year."

"Huh. Sounds an awful lot like you bandits got a sophisticated system of self-rule."

"Hell yeah, we do. Not to say we don't sometimes brawl amongst ourselves. Ain't nothing wrong with letting off some steam from time to time. Keeps them reflexes sharp and—Hey, that don't go there!" El Oso shouts at a pair of bandits setting up equipment on the other side of the stage. "Spider Sal! You see this? Straighten that mess out, or it's your head."

"If y'all get along so dang well," Sebastian says, as intrigued by this peek into bandit social structure as he is with whatever's coming together on the stage, "why let everybody think the crews are constantly at war with each other?"

"You wouldn't believe how many times some young Feudlander lordling, still wet behind the ears, decides the best way to make a name for himself is by offing one of the infamous bandit bosses. But they ain't never got the stones to do it themselves. They come to one of us to do it for them, thinking they're handing us some golden opportunity."

"But in reality, they're telling on themselves. Okay. That's actually pretty ingenious."

"Plus, they pay well, and in advance. Nothing in the code against easy loot."

Sebastian shakes his head, solemn. "What is this world coming to when a power-hungry warlord can't trust a merciless bandit boss? And the Feudlanders never catch on?"

"Them warlords ain't as good at communication and cooperation as us bandits."

"And I reckon ain't none of them too eager to broadcast their stupidity to their enemies."

"You ain't wrong."

"Well, Mr. Loco," Sebastian says, "this has been a fascinating and enlightening chat. Do you feel like we done grown close? 'Cuz I think we done grown close. Like, 'I ain't gonna kill you 'cuz I didn't get my way' close. Amiright?"

El Oso points a beefy finger in Sebastian's face. "I suggest you don't forget my advice about stupid risks."

"This is a fair competition. All you gotta do is be better than Sweetie."

"Just you wait," El Oso says, his grin wide.

"What's that supposed to mean?"

"You'll see, friend. You'll see."

El Oso strides off, laughing.

It's the sound of a guy who's sure he's got this thing in the bag.

SWEETIE LAUGHS. A lot.

That probably isn't the greatest sign that Sebastian's zany idea to try the direct approach will get him anywhere.

After she recovers, she restraps her holsters across her chest, strolls past Sebastian, and positions herself before the truck's big side-view mirror. She extracts a small tin from a pocket hidden within her ruffles. With the tiny brush and palette of colors inside the tin, she takes her time reapplying red to her lips.

He supposes that means that the make-out portion of their stolen time together has concluded. A necessary evil, he reminds himself as he watches her mouth brighten to the tempting tone of ripe berries.

Finally, she asks, with a satisfied pop of her lips, "Was it hellions?"

"Was what hellions?"

"The reason you need that arm?"

She returns the tin to the folds of her dress and pulls out a new one. This time, she runs the little brush over a black square and swipes her eyelashes.

Whatever she's using is different from the dark grease that so many bandits or even townsfolk on watch duty smudge around their eyes to help with the sun's glare. It reminds him of those whatchamacallits he's seen women using in Old World videos but never in real life.

"Or should I say, the reason somebody you care about needs that arm?" She turns to him, head tilted thoughtfully.

He looks away from her. A sour taste comes to his mouth. The memories tug at him, and he hurls his mind in the other direction. He is not going there. Not now. Not ever.

"Let me guess," she says. "You're doing this for a girl. Hoping to woo her with that thing? Is that how you'll prove your undying devotion?"

He tilts his head back and grins at her. "Do I spy the green eye of jealousy? And here I thought you wanted to use me up and toss me aside, a fate that I was determined to accept with a brave face, no matter how much heartache it would inevitably cause me in the end."

She studies him a moment longer, painted lips pursed. "So not hellions, but it was definitely some type of monster."

Returning her attention to the mirror, she resumes the work on her lashes.

"I'll tell you this much..." he says.

"Yes?"

"Since I'm obviously more than a boy toy to you, it's only fair that I confess something, Miss Skull Crusher." He plops down onto a row of orphaned bench seats. "I, too, have given a fair amount of thought as to our long and blissfully happy future together."

"It musta been sludgebrains."

"Now, I do like to travel, and I know you'll be busy running a merciless bandit crew and whatnot, but I reckon we could make it work. It might be nice having a home base for a change."

"No, not sludgebrains." She turns back to him, eyes wide. Impressed. With three categories of monster out there preying on mankind, the process of elimination has led her to the only answer left. "Damn. You know somebody who survived a flatliner raid?"

He forces his clenched fists to relax. Forces out the breath trapped in his lungs. Forces nonchalance by lying back on the bench, hands folded beneath his head.

"If we have a girl—and hear me out—whaddya think about the name Sebastianina Skull Crusher Hyphen Yun?" he says. "Sounds regal, don't it?"

"Aah, you survived it too. You just got a little more interesting, pretty boy."

"We'll call our son Sweetario of course. It's only fair to you."

"Who'd they take from you?"

"Or maybe Sweetarius? Which do you reckon'll strike more fear in the hearts of his enemies?"

Her tin clinks shut. Seconds later, she's standing over him, brandishing a cold smile. "You always go so far out of your way to avoid talking about this?"

His easy smile hardens into a grimace. She isn't wrong. He hasn't just buried that day deep, deep in the recesses of his mind. He's built a labyrinth around that section of his memories, so twisted and confusing and full of misleading non sequiturs and distracting pop culture references that even David Bowie in a codpiece would think it's excessive.

Going where Sweetie is trying to drive them will never be easy or straightforward.

"Now, how am I expected to answer your question if you ain't gonna answer mine?" she says.

He sits up, grips the edge of the seat, but he resists the urge to bolt from this conversation and the uncomfortable direction she's steered them despite his best efforts. He does need an answer from her, and somehow, he has to convince her to give him the one he wants.

"Everybody done survived something," he says, forcing his lips into a grin. "Don't really matter, do it? All you need to know is Betty belongs to someone pretty freakin' awesome. I wouldn't be alive if it weren't for her. And she wouldn't need a prosthetic arm if it weren't for me."

Sweetie moves in close, bringing him eye to eye with the soft yellow fabric and hard leather holster strapped over her midsection.

Her touch explores the planes of his cheeks and the angle of his jaw before settling at the base of his skull. Her fingers twine through the tiny hairs on the nape of his neck.

Sebastian's arms find their way around her waist all on their own accord. His fingers play up and down the smooth, soft fabric covering the small of her back. She feels like luxury.

"When me and my brother were little," she says, "our dad, Hawk, was betrayed by his own lieutenant. Slit his throat clean through and took over his crew. Did it right in front of us, too, like we weren't of no consequence whatsoever.

"And just like that, everything changed. No dad. No family. No home. Woulda lost our lives, too, but we were smart enough to get out of there before the blood cooled.

"We spent years singing for our supper down in the Feudlands. First on dirt roads, then in fancy parlors, and then big ol' opulent ballrooms. All that time, I never lost sight of why I fought to keep going. Why I trained nonstop. Got stronger, faster, smarter."

With one hand, she pulls out a necklace tucked into her dress. A clunky charm dangles at the end of the chain. She holds it up for him to see.

Only it's not like any charm Sebastian's ever seen. Fleshy and shriveled and the polar opposite of appealing. It doesn't exactly coordinate well with her yellow flounces.

"Six months ago," she says, grinning down at him, still tenderly running her finger through the small hairs at the back of his neck, "I cut Blade's lying tongue from his mouth and strung it on a chain."

Sebastian freezes. A shiver runs through him. One very different from what her earlier touch had elicited.

"Oh, darn," he says. "Now what'll I get you for your birthday?"

"After I let that snake take in the sight of me wearing his tongue like a pretty little charm, I looked him dead in the eye as I carved that disloyal heart of his right out of his chest. I think Daddy woulda been proud."

"I mean, yeah. What father wouldn't be?"

"This world ain't no kinder to kids than it is to adults. But me and you, we're the same."

"Well, I ain't cut my mortal enemy's tongue from their mouth. Yet. But who knows what the future holds?"

She chuckles and brushes a long strand of black hair away from his face. "Sebastian, we send this cruel, ugly world a great big 'screw you' by doing more than surviving. We do right by those who mean something to us."

"I gotta admit, I may have been called selfish on occasion. I don't know if I deserve to be put in the same category as you."

"Ain't nothing wrong with doing what makes us happy, and sometimes, doing right can be just the thing for it."

"So you're saying this is your definition of happy?" He hooks a finger through the chain around her neck. Without touching the gross, shriveled thing that used to be a tongue, of course.

She smiles. "And I won't apologize for it."

"You are terrifying."

"I know."

Logic would suggest he steer clear of this beautiful, deadly woman.

He tugs her even closer. She slips onto his lap and leans into the kiss. Unlike their earlier frantic meeting of lips, they savor each other this time, unhurried.

What has logic ever really done for anybody?

"Miss Skull Crusher," Sebastian says when they part, just so. "I was sweet on you from the first second I laid eyes on you, but I reckon I might actually like you."

"I could see myself getting used to having you around."

"So now that we done bonded over sob stories, have I warmed the cockles of your cold, bandit heart? Will you let me have that arm? Assuming you win."

"Of course not."

He can't exactly say he's surprised. Asking for it outright had been a long shot at best. But still…

"Aw, c'mon, Sweetie. You and me are totally having a thing. Don't ruin the moment. I know I ain't got much to offer, but if you let me have it, I'll make it up to you in whatever way you see fit."

"I'll be the first to admit you got a talented tongue, Sebastian Yun—"

"I do aim to please."

"But even you can't talk fast enough to convince me to give up that prize."

"What if I take back that thing I said about not seducing you to get what I want?"

She throws her head back in a laugh. "I know I make it look easy, but taking control of one of the biggest crews out there ain't a walk in the shade. Plenty of my people remember my dad and that he didn't deserve how Blade did him dirty. But plenty more were loyal to the backstabbing bastard. I done spent months purging my ranks.

"That cybernetic arm is worth more than anything else in the Midlands. Maybe even the Feudlands. It ain't mine to give away. My crew wants a win, and I aim to give 'em exactly that."

"I don't suppose a shout-out to the Bashers on my show could be considered a win?"

"I wish I could help you out here. I really do."

He sighs, dropping his forehead to her shoulder. "I get it. Had to try."

"Sure."

Her fingers resume tracing circles in the small hairs at the nape of his neck. His eyes flutter closed.

"That feels real good, by the way," he says. "It's like a little massage, and believe it or not, the day's been kinda stressful."

She laughs again. "We can stay here a little while longer if you'd like."

"Yes, please."

She indulges him in comfort and silence for maybe a full minute, her fingers drawing continuous, soothing circles.

"Oh, and Sebastian…"

"Hmm?"

"There's no 'assuming' anything. I am winning this here contest. I know I'm the best thing to hit that stage. That arm," she says quietly, "is already mine."

He tenses under her soft touch, straightens off her shoulder. Sweetie cups his chin in her hands, holding his gaze.

"If I hear so much as a whisper that you tried making the same deal with El Oso or Ruthless, I will sever your head from your neck." She pulls him in for a kiss as sweet as her name, whispering before their lips meet, "You believe me, don't you?"

·⸱·╵╷╵╷╵·╷╵╵╷╵╷╵╷╵·╷╵·╷╵·⸱·

IT'S after the intermission and after he's been threatened by two out of three bandit bosses, and Sebastian can't believe what he's seeing.

El Oso had promised a showstopper. And apparently, that means smoke machines, lasers, and backup dancers. Backup dancers who, by the way, are lowered from rigging somehow attached to the stage's high scaffolding.

This is why it had taken so long for the Wild Raiders to set up their gear. Much of which must have been custom-built.

El Oso's voice isn't as impressive as Sweetie's, but he belts out Led Zepplin's "A Whole Lotta Love" like the song was written for him, for this moment.

From her lofty seat among her entourage, Sweetie yawns widely and pretends to fall asleep.

But the audience loves every minute of the spectacle before them. Even as the performance stretches on for a Full. Twenty. Minutes. El Oso's energy never fades, and neither does the crowd's enthusiasm.

For the finale, fire shoots out over the heads of the frenzied crowd while El Oso—whose backup dancers had smoothly attached him to a harness— ascends into the air with arms stretched wide.

The cheers and applause of the crowd seem to last as long as the marathon performance. The Feudlander piano man collapses against his keys, exhausted.

Sebastian sits back in his seat, awed. And a little more than devastated.

Code or no code, El Oso knew he didn't need to swipe the arm because he was guaranteed to steal the show. No way will he accept defeat, regardless of how amazing Sweetie had been in her own right.

Sebastian makes the mistake of glancing toward her. She smiles sweetly and drags a slow finger across her throat. The gesture is so subtle it might have been mistaken for coy flirting.

As if he'd forgotten her chilling threat. Or El Oso's.

His head's relationship with his body has never felt so tenuous.

"Oh, crap!" Sebastian cries, horrified. "He's good. Really, really good."

9

Sebastian collapses on his disheveled bed, face-first. With his eyes shut, the world spins even more unsteadily.

Grace's knock on his door is accompanied by the music of clay beads clacking against each other. The sound drags him back to another life, memories he left behind a long time ago.

He isn't leaving his room as long as she's out there.

If he opens that door, he'll have to see her face. And if he sees her face, he'll have to get mad. And if he gets mad at her, he'll have to feel guilty about it. And he's not in the mood for that emotional turmoil. So he does the reasonable thing and ignores her knocks.

Right. Like she'll think he isn't home and go away.

Of all the Hopeful bands out there, they had to run into hers.

When Grace left Sebastian to rejoin the Congregation of Hope, she hadn't asked him if he was okay with it. She told him she was going back. That was that.

Had her announcement shocked him?

In all the time that it was just the two of them, she continued to wear that one string of blue and white faith beads around her neck every single day. They were a part of her. She prayed every night before bed and at the start of every meal. She lost herself in the study of scriptures.

No. It hadn't been a shock when she left.

It was the day he had dreaded from the moment she became the one person who meant everything to him.

There's a soft rustle against the door. Sebastian pictures her leaning back against it, sliding to the floor. She'll be absently worrying beads between her thumb and forefinger. She never knew what to do with her hand when it wasn't busy.

"I like your friends." Her voice is muffled through the door.

"You can have 'em," he mutters into his pillow, not loud enough for her to hear. Because he isn't talking to her. Eventually, she'll get the message and go away.

"Meza's a bit aloof, and Scott's... different..."

"Heh. If only you knew."

"But they're nice."

"Too nice, apparently."

The bus had been locked up tight when he left earlier in the day. The only way Grace could've been waiting inside HRM was if Meza let her in.

"Her Royal Majesty looks amazing," she continues, oblivious to his side of the conversation. "I can't believe you did all this by yourself. Musta taken forever."

It had taken over a year to whip the interior into a halfway livable condition and get the engine running reliably enough to go farther than a mile. Even then, it was prone to shutting down without warning or not starting up at all, stranding him wherever he happened to be for days, weeks at a time. It was Meza showing up that really got the bus moving. But he was basically practically mostly done by then. So she can't take too much of the credit.

"Don't be too hard on Meza for letting me in here," Grace says. "I made a very compelling case. Mentioned a few things you do that only someone who's spent a ton of time with you would know. Like how when you're really into a task, you sing everything you're doing to the beat of 'Stayin' Alive.'"

"It's the perfect song for that sorta thing!" He's still talking to his pillow and not her.

"Or how you sometimes have whole conversations with yourself when you sleep," Grace says. "By the way, Meza agrees that it's creepy. I reckon even your listeners don't know them parts of you. Which may be for the best."

In his mind, he can see the way her eyebrow arches when she teases him, the corner of her mouth lifting in a tiny half grin.

"Would it make you feel a smidge better to know Meza disabled steering?" Grace says. "And threatened to hunt me down if I try anything that makes her regret trusting me?"

That sounds more like the Meza he knows. And yes, it does make him feel a smidge better.

"Tell me you been taking care of yourself, Baz. Can't you at least say that much?"

His own question dies on the tip of his tongue. There's no point in asking. He already knows she won't go with him when he leaves.

"'Course I listen to your show," she says. "I never miss an episode if I can help it. But that don't mean I ain't been missing you. That I ain't been missing those nights we'd stay up way too late talking about everything, and nothing."

Sebastian flops onto his back, arms and legs akimbo.

"Don't excuse her," he whispers to the stains in the ceiling even though they're being super rude and refusing to hold still. "People gotta be held accountable for their bad decisions."

The stains laugh at him, saying, *You're one to talk.*

"Who asked you?" he hisses back.

Grace falls silent. She shifts against the door. Is she straining to hear? Had he spoken too loudly? He smooshes his pillow over his face.

"I knew you wouldn't want to see me," she says eventually, "but I just… I had to try. 'Cuz I even been missing that stupid, smug look I could never make you wipe off your face."

He rolls his lips together. He won't say another word, refuses to give her any hope that they can go back to the way things used to be between them. They sailed way past that point the day she chose the Congregation of Hope.

"I guess I'll go." There's more shuffling and the soft clinking of beads. She must be getting up. "But remember I love you, Baz. Nothing will ever change that."

Sebastian listens to her footsteps pad down the aisle. He tells himself he's relieved that she's leaving. He should be relieved. His ghosts are better off staying in the past, and she awakens the worst of his phantoms.

With a groan, he picks himself off the bed and drags his feet to the door. When he steps out, Grace is already at the stairs on the other end of the aisle. Head swimming, he props an arm against the steadying doorframe.

There are plenty of empty bunks hugging either side of the aisle. She could have her pick of any of them. Hell, he'd let her have the master suite if it meant carrying her away from those blue flags.

He dismisses the futile thought.

"What happened to your arm?" he asks.

He doesn't mean the fact that one of her arms is missing. He hardly remembers her ever having the one she'd been born with. But her right sleeve shouldn't be empty, folded and pinned to keep it out of the way. He'd noticed it right away when he first saw her downstairs. Telling himself he didn't care about it hadn't worked.

"Well…" She bites her lip, looks away. Sebastian already knows he won't like what she's going to say.

He lets out an exasperated sigh. "I won't get mad. I promise."

"Yes, you will, but I guess at least you're talking to me, and I can't resist that." She paces toward him. "A couple of days ago, a group of bandits came into camp. Some of them were injured. Nothing too serious. I helped see to their wounds, and we let them stay the night. I took Betty off before going to bed, like I usually do. And the next morning, it was gone."

Grace throws her hand up, palm out, an attempt to hold back the tidal wave of anger that no doubt flashes across his expression.

"There you go, not getting mad," she says. "Just breathe, Baz. It's okay."

He grits his teeth, takes the advised deep breath before asking, "How? How is it okay?"

"I know you went through a lot of trouble to get it and all. And I am grateful. But I was fine all them years without a super, high-tech cybernetic arm. I'll be fine now. Who knows? Maybe there's somebody out there who needs it more than I do."

"You sound like a freakin' Hopeful."

"Because I am a freakin' Hopeful. Which means I don't regret helping them bandits out, even if I lost something because of it."

"And next time, when it's your life you lose?"

"Then I reckon it means I've fulfilled my purpose for being in this world and get to spend eternity with the Lord I love."

"God, this is why—" He clamps his mouth shut before he says something he'll regret. His fists are balled so tightly that, at any minute now, his palms will start dripping blood.

He's not getting mad. He's not getting mad. He is not getting mad.

And not only because he'd promised. He already knows it's a useless reaction where she's concerned. It doesn't change anything. All it manages to do is leave him feeling drained.

She places a hand on his arm. Her touch is warm, familiar. He's grown since the last time they stood this close. If he were to hug her, she might get lost in his arms.

"Everything works out the way it should," she says.

"Which crew was it?"

"It don't matter."

"If it was a couple of days ago, you musta still been in Black Raven territory. Not like a Hopeful caravan covers a ton of ground in a day."

"Really, Baz, it's o—"

"I'm gonna get it back."

"From bandits?"

"Yeah."

"You're drunk."

"Yeah. But I'm gonna get it back."

"The Congregation is packing up in the morning."

"I'll find you."

She wants to protest. He can tell. Same as he'd been able to tell that she'd wanted to give him a hard time about going into an Intelli-City by himself after he first gave her the arm. She knows him well enough to understand that telling him not to do something only results in him doing it sooner, and more recklessly.

So after a pause, she simply says, "Okay."

"Grace…" He shuffles back into his room.

"Yeah."

"I miss you too."

10

AS THE BANDIT Queen takes to the stage, not only is Sebastian no closer to walking out of this place with Betty the Cybernetic Arm in his possession, but two of the crew bosses have made it perfectly clear that choosing the wrong winner will result in his immediate demise.

Not exactly what he'd call progress.

Ruthless takes to the stage with no fanfare. Mic in hand, she glares at the audience. The Black Ravens scream and cheer for their intrepid leader. The other crews are noticeably subdued, restraining from the usual jeers and heckling, which they hadn't held back on for the other singers. Even the other bosses had gotten their share of derision before their outstanding performances began.

This unruly crowd knows better than to cross Ruthless. The other bosses smirk and roll their eyes, but they have no huge displays of disrespect for her like they had for either other. So even the other bosses hesitate to get on her bad side.

Everyone is so scared of her she could probably announce that the sky is purple, and no one would call her on it.

Sebastian straightens in his chair.

He chides himself. It's so obvious. Why didn't he realize the way out of this sooner?

If she were to win this thing, the other bosses might be angry, but they also might accept it.

And Ruthless is already willing to part with Betty. The fact that she's put it up as a prize is proof enough. Maybe he'll have better luck convincing her to let him have it than he had with Sweetie.

If a girl named Sweetie can be alarmingly ruthless, why can't a woman named Ruthless have a hidden sweet side?

Okay. It's a leap.

But he's stuck between a rock named El Oso and a hard place called Sweetie. A leap might be his last chance to avoid being crushed to death.

Ruthless just has to be as good on that stage as the other bosses were.

Maybe it's an inherent trait that to be a bandit boss, one must also—inexplicably—be an amazing performer. Maybe there's something about leading a band of cutthroats on bloody raids that ups one's knack for showmanship?

Ruthless raises her mic and nods to the piano man. He begins plucking out the distinctive melody of "Old Town Road."

Sebastian props his elbows on the table and folds his fingers together.

"C'mon, Big R," he whispers. A desperate prayer. "Wow me."

And boy, does she ever.

She's bad.

Like, terrible.

Like, worse than terrible.

Like, her notes aren't flat. They're concave.

Her voice has all the charm of a sharp nail dragging

across a rusty sheet of metal. Trying to fix the sounds coming from her mouth would break autotune. Like. As a concept. All of autotune would cease to exist. That awe-inspiring, domineering presence shrivels down to an unengaging, colorless shadow of herself.

It's painful to watch, and yet Sebastian can't look away.

The audience is uncomfortably silent. In shock, probably. Sebastian isn't the only one who hadn't expected her performance to be quite this *abysmal.* Sweetie and El Oso's faces are stuck somewhere between disbelief and horror.

When the song comes to its merciful end, tears of gratitude threaten to stream down Sebastian's cheeks. It's over. He has survived an experience against which all other horrors he's suffered pale in comparison.

And then, as Ruthless turns toward the judges' table, he remembers... he's not done yet. He's supposed to say something about that travesty he just witnessed.

Throughout his brief but bracing tenure as judge for this competition, Sebastian has prided himself on being able to toe the line. Even for contestants whose performances were a disaster, he managed to find some glimmer of redemption to mold into a compliment, even in an otherwise poor review.

But that won't work now. Ruthless gave him absolutely nothing to work with. If she'd dropped dead on the stage, at least he'd have been able to say, "You make an impressive corpse, ma'am."

The audience stirs from their stupor slowly. A single, slow clap rings through the dumbfounded silence. A trickle of applause joins in, then it builds to a defining crescendo. The bandits cheer for her like she's the second coming of Beyoncé.

They clap. They roar. They whistle. All of it's a little too enthusiastic. It's knife-to-the-throat praise.

In that moment, he wonders if his faith in charm and charisma has been wasted. All this time, he should've been cultivating a reputation based on fear and intimidation. The results speak for themselves.

"I think we know who the winner is," Bow Tie Bob says, having swooped up one of the extra judges' mics. There are plenty to spare. He sends a significant look to Sebastian, a lifeline.

El Oso throws up his hands, and Sweetie's smile twists into a grimace. That's their only protest. It's as Sebastian had hoped. They'll put up with Ruthless winning because they have to.

Ruthless raises the mic to her mouth. Without prompting, the audience quiets their clamor.

"Mr. Yun. Is this your judgment?"

"Of course," Bow Tie Bob says. The warning he casts couldn't be any clearer if it were written on a giant neon sign. "She's the clear winner. Right?"

Hundreds of eyes pivot to Sebastian, expectant.

"What can I say…" he starts, carefully.

Seriously.

What. Can. He. Say?

"That was…"

He should definitely lie.

She does not look like someone who takes criticism well.

Lie and live to see another day.

"I respect music too much to pretend that was anything but all-the-way awful," he says.

Or brutal honesty. That's also an option.

"In as literal a sense as possible, there was nothing redeeming about that torment you just forced upon us. Except for the fact that it eventually came to an end."

Why is he still talking?

"I honestly never knew that anyone could butcher a song

I love so badly that I may never be able to listen to it ever again. I done experienced a lot of truly horrible, nightmarish situations in my eighteen years on this earth, but it ain't until now that I been this emotionally scarred."

Why isn't anybody stopping him?

"Forget knives and blasters. Next time you raid an unsuspecting town, do everything you had the audacity to subject us to on that stage. Every one of them folks will gladly hand over everything they own, up to and including their firstborn child, to make it stop."

Someone. Anyone. Please, shove a sock in his mouth. Or a grenade.

"I know I should probably start begging for my life somewhere about now, but I'd rather beg you to never, ever do that again. For the sake of all that is holy, please, don't make anybody else suffer through that for as long as you live."

Every single member of the audience stares at Sebastian in disbelief. Jaws hang open. Eyes bulge. All except Meza. Face in her palm, she shakes her head. The entire shipyard is as silent as the death that surely awaits him.

"Sooo…" Sebastian's projected voice reverberates throughout the quiet, cavernous space. "Those are my thoughts. When you kill me, I'll thank you to make it quick and painless."

He pushes his mic away. Finally, he's managed to stanch the flow of word vomit spewing from his mouth.

Sebastian pulls the mic back. "Considering you already done tortured me today."

Okay. Now he's done.

And now that he's managed to get on the wrong side of three out of three judges, he's pretty sure he knows what happens next.

IT'S minutes before Sweetie attempts to give Sebastian his much-needed haircut, scalp and all.

Sebastian, Meza, and Scott Buddy crouch side by side behind the tall upright piano. Sebastian is all too aware of the fact that their extremely temporary cover won't last long against the screaming horde of weapon-wielding bandits descending upon them.

"So much for charm and charisma," Meza says, scanning the area for a weapon.

Sebastian pouts, indignant. "Hey, it got us pretty far! But let's be honest. I think we both knew it was gonna end like this."

As it would happen, it turns out that bandits have a thing for violence. Same as kindling has a thing for fire. It only takes the right spark. And a pissed-off bandit boss is just the strike of flint to ignite the inferno.

It took no time at all for the barely contained chaos of hundreds of bandits under one roof to erupt into the unleashed chaos of the aforementioned bandits shouting and screaming, punching and pushing, stabbing and shooting.

Wild Raiders versus Bashers versus Black Ravens versus Wild Raiders. Most of them are probably too drunk to even ask why they're fighting, assuming they needed a reason even when sober.

And then, of course, there are those with a clear purpose. To do as their boss lady commanded and "get" Sebastian and his friends.

"It's clear that one of us should nobly sacrifice ourself so the others can get away." Sebastian raises an eyebrow at Scott Buddy.

"Help me with this." Meza has twisted around. She tugs at one of the thick wooden slats holding up the sturdy piano frame.

Scott Buddy tears it away easily and hands it over.

"Ooh! Me too! I want one too!" Sebastian says as Meza grips the slat in both hands and practices a swing.

But before the sludgebrain can use its monster strength to rip off another slat, the piano is yanked away by the small troop of Bashers that have finally converged on their targets.

Meza pops to her feet. Her makeshift club arcs through the air. A big bruiser who doesn't need to get any uglier catches a face full of pain. Her strike connects with all the force she can muster.

The looming bandits think better of getting too close. Their grips on their weapons tighten in anticipation of taking any opening they can get. After all, what chance does one teenage girl with one wooden slat stand against their chains, blades, clubs, and spiking brass knuckles?

A glint of motion flashes in Sebastian's periphery. Nearly two decades of reacting on instinct in life-or-death situations kicks in.

He twists backward and out of the path of a wickedly sharp ax. It misses his nose by an inch. He wishes he could say this is the first time a girl he's been amorous with has tried to kill him.

Or that it'll be the last.

Before he can regain his balance, Sweetie, with her endless supply of wickedly sharp axes, lunges toward him. She brandishes an ax in each hand and a smile turned manic with rage.

Sebastian succumbs to the pull of gravity, slamming into the rough surface of the stage. He rolls, not giving himself the chance to catch his breath. Sweetie slices savagely through the air. Her blade cuts through the empty space where his head had been only a millisecond earlier.

His dark hair may be in need of a haircut, but that trim would've been way too close.

"Wait!" Sebastian tosses up his inexcusably empty hands, placating.

Sweetie pauses. She twirls an ax, the motion fluid and well-practiced. "You really think you can talk your way out of this?"

Sebastian offers his most disarming grin. "You said it yourself, I got a talented tongue. Which is why I reckon you wouldn't wanna go and do anything regretful to the wielder of such an outstanding talent."

She cocks her head. "I've had better."

"You're just saying that to hurt me."

"No. The axes are for hurting you."

Sebastian scrambles out of the way. Her blades are a deadly whirl that nearly slices his head clean off.

Around him, everything is chaos. Dozens, probably hundreds, of similar skirmishes have broken out across the shipyard.

On the other side of the crowded stage, Meza squares off against three rough-looking men. Each one is taller, wider, and more muscled than her. One blows a kiss as they circle her. She extends a thick wooden slat before her like a club.

Between Sebastian and Meza, Scott Buddy moves with freaky, boneless grace, easily dodging assaults from multiple attackers despite cradling Betty the Cybernetic Arm. But it doesn't fight back. Not a single punch or kick or swipe of retractable claws.

What's the point of secretly traveling with a creature of unspeakable evil if it doesn't unleash unholy hell at times that are convenient for Sebastian?

"Hey, parasite—" Sebastian narrowly avoids a blow that would've deprived him of a left hand. "Now would be a really good time to go all *aaargh!*"

Several bandits come at Scott Buddy from different directions. The sludgebrain leaps clear over the heads of

Meza and her opponents to land on the upright piano. "We are making promise."

"Ain't you heard?" Sebastian says. "Promises are meant to be broken."

Meza, Sebastian notices, is now on her biggest opponent's back, the makeshift club pulled tight across his veiny neck. At some point when Sebastian's attention was otherwise occupied, she'd dropped her two other attackers.

"We are not breaking."

Sebastian growls in frustration. Why did Scott Buddy have to go and make such a stupid promise?

"I told you what would happen if you crossed me!" Sweetie calls out. She's traded her smaller throwing ax for longer ones meant for hand-to-hand combat.

"You were serious?" Sebastian says. "I thought for sure you were playing."

Sweetie's attacks pick up speed. She's a whirlwind of fury and blades. Sebastian stops trying to keep up with how Meza and Scott are doing. He doesn't have an ounce of focus to spare. His feet are in constant motion. He bobs and weaves. Dances out of her reach and twists just in time. But with so many bodies in frantic motion, jamming up the small space, he's pressed back into her danger zone again and again.

A glimpse of metal on the ground catches his attention.

Sebastian tucks, rolls, and springs back to his feet with the fallen mic stand in his grip. Pretty impressive maneuver, if he does say so himself.

Now, when Sweetie strikes, he stands his ground. Her ax clashes against the metal rod. The reverberations of metal clanging against metal tingle Sebastian's palms.

He blocks again and again, but it's all he can do to defend himself. She gives him no time to recover from her attacks.

An ax crashes against the stand again. This time, the blade hooks behind the metal pole.

Her smirk brightens. Eyes flash with triumph.

"Oh, crap," Sebastian says a second before she pulls on her ax, ripping his only defense from his hands.

"That all you got?" She circles him, ax twirling, a predator savoring the last moment before she sinks her teeth into her prey.

"You know," Sebastian huffs, trying to catch his breath. He raises his hands, palms out. "I ain't much of a hand-to-hand guy, but I am nothing less than awe-inspiring when I got my blasters."

"Silly boy, bandits know better than to rely on blasters only."

"I can see the wisdom in that."

She lunges.

They dance once again.

As Sebastian's exhaustion catches up to him, making his steps slower and sloppier, she somehow seems to get faster and sharper. The surety of her quickly approaching victory spurs her.

Sebastian loses his footing, falls back.

There's no hesitation in Sweetie. She comes in for the kill.

He can only brace himself.

The final, fatal strike never comes.

Ruthless is there, blocking the blow with her sturdy poleax. It's only a million times more impressive than the sad mic stand Sebastian had been using to defend himself.

The stage is more crowded than ever. The number of occupants has doubled. The slew of newcomers, all bearing the distinctive raven-and-thorns tattoo, go to town on the Bashers.

Meza and Scott Buddy ease out of their defensive stances, their many dancing partners having been stolen by Wild Raiders.

Ruthless and Sweetie tango. Sweetie is a force of nature,

her rhythm wild and unpredictable. Ruthless is control incarnate. Her precise movements waste neither time nor energy.

Their tango takes them to the end of the stage. Sweetie spares only a cursory glance at the short drop at her back before launching herself, roaring, at Ruthless.

With two clean motions of the bladed end of her poleax, Ruthless divests Sweetie of one ax then the other.

A growl of pure hatred erupts from Sweetie. She reaches for one of her smaller throwing axes, but Ruthless thrusts with the blunt end of her weapon. Sweetie tumbles off the stage with a rage-filled shriek.

Ruthless turns to Sebastian, still on the ground and utterly stunned. The Wild Raiders have pushed the Bashers toward the edges of the stage, if not off it entirely.

"Come with me," Ruthless says.

She strides toward the back of the stage and through the black backdrop curtains. Her Wild Raiders clear a path as she moves. She doesn't look back to see if Sebastian, Meza, or Scott Buddy are following.

It's a foregone conclusion.

···||||||||·|···|||||||·|·|||····

AFTER SEBASTIAN'S less-than-generous critique of her performance, Ruthless says nothing.

For way too long.

Her intense, stifling gaze is trained on no one but Sebastian.

He freezes, holding his breath like a startled animal who thinks, *If I don't move, maybe that big, scary predator won't see me.* His mind races.

Is this a silent threat?

No, he'd know if she was threatening him.

Right?

Actually, he'd probably be dead already if she intended to kill him.

Or maybe she's deciding exactly how to do him in.

How best to make an example of him for humiliating her in front of everyone.

Although it's hardly fair that she'd come after him for that. She'd embarrassed herself first.

Abruptly, Ruthless turns from him. She descends from the stage and returns to her seat without saying another word.

Sebastian lets out a breath he's been holding for a lifetime.

"That's what I'm talking about, kid!" El Oso bellows. "Wouldna guessed a scrawny fellow like you had the balls. Now, go ahead and name me the winner so we can all go home."

"Excuse me." The youngest boss's tone is sickly sweet but strong and clear. "What makes you think you're going home with my prize?"

"Looky here, little girl. Your performance was cute. I'll give you that. But you ain't no match for me. I am a master of the craft. At best, you're a one-hit wonder."

"It's adorable you think your words mean anything to me, old man, when all that matters is what our judge here decides. Go on, Sebastian. Let them know I'm the winner."

Everyone's attention lands on Sebastian like a fifty-ton rock. He knows there's a way out of this mess. His thoughts zoom through his head at a million miles per hour, too fast and jumbled to be of any use.

Sweetie unsheathes an ax, runs her thumb along its blade. "Speak up, Sebastian. We can't hear you."

El Oso throws his massive, well-worn club over his shoulder. "Spit it out already, Sebastian Yun."

The grumbling of the audience rises to a shout. Sebastian can't make out the individual threats issuing from the crowd of bandits, but he gets the gist of it all.

Choose Sweetie, he dies. Choose El Oso, he dies. He didn't choose Ruthless, he should definitely die.

Dammit, charm and charisma. Where are they when he really needs them?

The song starts out quiet. Unsure.

Bit by bit, as everyone slowly notices the unexpected contestant, the din simmers down to a murmur.

Scott stands in the center of the stage, mic gripped in both hands, eyes closed. With each bar it sings, its voice grows louder, powerful. More confident.

When it opens its eyes, Scott seems to be looking beyond this place and this time. It's not singing to this crowd. It's reaching out for someone, somewhere very far from here.

Quiet descends over the audience. Not just silence. Breathlessness. Like every person in the shipyard is afraid of breaking the spell Scott casts with his clear, effortlessly powerful voice.

He sings about missing home, about not knowing when he'll see it again. Not knowing where he'll be tomorrow, only that it's far from where he wishes he could be.

He sings of the dusty road. The sleet and rain. The sun kisses another day full of longing and the pain of hope.

He sings of his despair that he'll never see home again.

Sebastian presses his eyes closed, pushes against the pressure building against the back of his lids.

The faintest of memories brush against a part of himself that's been buried deep.

Squinting into the sun at a tall silhouette that reaches out to him. Falling asleep with his head on a soft lap, fabric tickling his nose. A song, hummed absently. The soft clacking of beds. A crooked smile. Feeling small but safe.

When Scott's last note fades, the audience's silence lingers. It's as if everyone is surprised to find themselves back in the here and now. The person they'd been holding, the place they'd been reliving, the feeling they'd remembered is gone.

And they'll never get it back again.

When the audience explodes into applause, it's loud enough to blow the roof off the place.

Eyes in the audience glisten. More than one face is streaked with tears. El Oso's lip trembles. Sweetie's hand finds her brother's. Ruthless watches the siblings, her expression unreadable.

It's the rarest gift of all. More than a great voice or stage presence. Scott possesses the ability to pull an entire audience from their bodies and carry them to a place that exists for only those few precious minutes.

To shift something inside a person and make them feel, even if just for a moment, every raw emotion he puts into the song.

Realizing he's been gaping since the song ended, Sebastian clamps his jaw shut. He brushes away an itchy tickle on his cheeks, and his fingers come away wet.

On Ruthless's platform, Meza presses her mouth into a straight line. Her gaze meets Sebastian's. For a second, it's like Sebastian is seeing a different person. He tilts his head, questioning. Her lips part like she wants to say something.

He's reminded very suddenly that he knows very little about his traveling companion. Her life before they met each other is a mystery. Another orphan. Another survivor. Another person on this planet with a tragic backstory they don't care to talk about.

She looks away.

Shaking his head to clear it, Sebastian returns to the situation before him. He leaps to his feet and bounces over to Scott.

"What was that, Scott?" He claps the kid on the shoulder and gives him an excited shake. "That was—You're amazing!"

Scott blinks, coming out of his own trance.

"We are Buddy," it corrects quietly.

Sebastian recoils, snatching his hand away. He catches himself mid-action, and his hand sort of hangs there between them as if confused.

Grabbing the mic from the stand, Sebastian turns away from him—it. Whatever. No time to re-examine his well-founded biases against monsters.

"I think you'll all agree," Sebastian tells the audience, "that performance deserves to be crowned winner!"

The crowd roars.

"Meza, why don't you bring this young man, who we definitely don't know, his prize?"

Ruthless offers a curt nod of approval. Meza doesn't hesitate. She grabs the arm and beelines for the stage.

"Liar!" Sweetie jumps to her feet then points an accusing ax and a poisonous smile toward Sebastian. "You know him. I saw you talking to that weirdo earlier."

"Oh," Sebastian remembers, belatedly. "Yeah."

"They're trying to fix this thing!" Sweetie says. "That arm belongs to me, and everybody here knows it!"

"Does it, now?" El Oso rises to his full, towering height. "And what did you do for Sebastian that makes you so sure you should get it? Maybe I'll let you convince me like you convinced him."

The lewd gesture that accompanies this statement… well, let's just say it's no surprise that Sweetie's brother whips out his big ol' battle axes and charges at El Oso. Tom leaps from Sweetie's platform to Ruthless's to El Oso's, where his swing of an ax slams into El Oso's raised club.

But maybe the scuffle between Tom and El Oso could have been squashed. Maybe the reckless, drunken merriment would have continued far into the night without turning into a giant melee.

The problem is Sweetie notices Sebastian ushering Meza, Scott Buddy, and Betty the Cybernetic Arm off the stage. With all eyes on Tom and El Oso, it seems as good a time as any to get scarce.

Miss Skull Crusher is of a different mind.

"Where do you think you're going with my prize?" she sings out pleasantly.

"Smoke break?" Sebastian offers.

"Your life or that arm," Sweetie says. "I can take one or both."

"What about the code? No stealing from bandits!"

"You declared your friend there the winner and rightful owner of that arm. Last I checked, he ain't no bandit."

Then she utters two words that guarantee all-out chaos.

"Get 'em."

And thus, the spark was lit and flung into the giant pile of kindling.

It's not only Bashers coming after Sebastian and his jolly gang. Or Tom's giant axes colliding against El Oso Loco's enormous club.

Everyone wants in on the action. They hardly seem to care who they're clashing against as long as they have a face to smash or knee to break. Wild Raiders. Bashers. Black Ravens. They all dance to the soundtrack of shouting and scrapping, screaming and bones crunching, weapons clashing and blasters firing.

Meza and Sebastian dive behind the poor shelter of the piano as the Bashers rush the stage. Meza leaps back into the open and returns a second later with Scott Buddy, who, as far as Sebastian could tell, thought standing out in the open is just the way to receive a murderous horde.

The bespectacled Feudlander crawls around the giant instrument to join them, cowering for dear life.

Sebastian gives him a disappointed look. "Listen, piano man, anybody with an ounce of survival instinct might think this would be an opportune time for a guy in your position to make a run for freedom. What with everybody distracted by trying to kill me and my associates."

The ingrate doesn't even have the courtesy to throw a thank-you over his shoulder before scampering off. They must not have home training in the Feudlands.

"So much for charm and charisma," Meza says, scanning the area for a weapon.

Sebastian pouts, indignant. "Hey, it got us pretty far! But let's be honest. I think we both knew it was gonna end like this."

11

When Sebastian slouches out of Her Royal Majesty, Betty the Cybernetic Arm hanging from the crook of his elbow, he's already made up his mind to enter the Congregation of Hope camp.

But his feet aren't quite convinced.

They won't move out of HRM's protective shadow.

Those flapping blue-and-white flags aren't very far away. A two-minute walk. That's all it is. Just one step in front of the other through the open gate of those mobile walls.

But, well, when his feet pivot and carry him back through HRM's back door, what can he do? They are, apparently, running the show today. And they are of the opinion that he doesn't have to do this. Who is he to argue?

He'll send Meza inside with the arm. Even if it means being on the receiving end of one of her lethal glares as she reminds him that she isn't his errand girl.

Or maybe she'll ask why he can't do it himself. He'll laugh it off, give her some witty BS answer. And she'll see right through him.

This one time, avoidance isn't an option.

On his second attempt, a constant stream of curses leap from his tongue as he crosses the short divide. He makes it within three feet of the camp before he doubles over and retches into a conveniently located scraggly bush.

Amid the airy, white tents of the camp, Sebastian is a dark cloud.

He doesn't meet any of these idiots' eyes as he trudges forward. He returns none of the cheerful greetings. Laughter and conversation and clacking of beads buzz all around him. He blocks it all out.

From the orderly layout to the rhythm of activity to the savory aroma of the food, all Congregation of Hope camps are the same. And somehow, it's still a part of him, in the way that some dreams—or nightmares—refuse to be fully forgotten. The familiarity of it all hits him like a punch to the gut.

But it's the soundtrack of the camp that truly threatens to drag him down. The constant flapping and cracking of those flags in the wind. The soft but pervasive tinkling of beads knocking together. The humming of a hymn, the lyrics of which somehow worm into his mind, unbidden, though he hasn't heard them in ten years.

Sebastian takes a long breath, reminds himself that he's only got to do this one thing. Then he can get out of here and back to the open road.

He should've sent Meza in.

Grace is right where Sebastian suspected she'd be. The school tent is open on all sides to let the breeze flow through. It's a small group of kids gathered for today's lesson. Smaller probably than it had been when the Hopefuls pulled up to the town of Vigilance a few days ago.

There are always plenty of orphans in need of shelter in the Midlands, and the Congregation of Hope collects every one they come across. But little kids never stay with the camps for long.

The towns of the Midlands might not let Hopefuls past their walls, but no one ever denies young orphans a safe place to call home. And since everyone knows flatliners only come in adult size, there's no harm in taking in children.

These kids in the school tent must be the children of Hopefuls. They would have no safe place to call home, not unless they turned out smarter than their parents and got the hell out of Dodge first chance they got.

Grace doesn't notice Sebastian's approach, absorbed in her lesson.

"Who can say condensation?" she asks.

"Con-din-say-shun," the kids parrot back with varying degrees of success. They're crowded around a small table that holds a half-empty water jar. They peer at it as if it's the most fascinating thing they've ever seen.

"The air we done sealed in the jar," Grace explains, "is warm and moist 'cuz of the hot water we put in there and trapped with the plate. Now, that there ice on top of the plate helps the moisture in the air condense and form little water droplets. Can you all see them?"

The kids ooh and aah over the miracle in a jar.

"This here's the same thing that happens when it rains, except that it goes on much, much, much higher in the atmosphere."

"Miss Grace!" A little hand shoots in the air. "I'm gonna put the whole world in a jar. Then we'll have rain all the time!"

Grace's mouth pulls into a crooked grin. "You're onto something, Penny, but I ain't sure switching out lack of rain for lack of oxygen is the best trade-off. Besides, the Lord provides. We might not have a lot of rain, but we get enough."

And that's about enough for Sebastian. Without a word, he drops Betty the Cybernetic Arm on the table. Grace and the kids jump at the heavy *thud*. He's walking away before she can recover from her surprise.

"Why don't you run off, kids?" she says behind him. "Tomorrow, we'll talk about thunder and lightning."

The children revert into play mode, laughing and teasing each other as they bounce past Sebastian. Not a care in the world.

"Baz, wait!"

He turns but doesn't step toward her. Her weight shifts as if she wants to close the distance between them.

She looks down at Betty, lays a hand on the forearm. "Can't say you don't know how to make an entrance."

"It's a gift," he says flatly.

He looks back toward the gates, glances toward the ground, shoves his hands into his pockets, then finally drags his gaze to her face. Seeing her in the flesh is so much harder sober.

Their eyes meet, but almost immediately flit away from each other. She bites her lips, holding back whatever she wants to say. It's unlike her.

Around them, it's business as usual throughout the camp, the Hopefuls going about their everyday tasks. The murmur of conversation, the hum of song, the trickling of laughter floats around the ill-fitting bubble that has enveloped Sebastian and Grace.

"I'm gonna—"

"This is pretty big—"

Their words jumble together, both of them talking at the same time.

"What—"

"You go—"

Another start and stop that manages to be both in and out

of sync at the same time. Sebastian gestures for Grace to speak first.

"This is pretty big." She speaks carefully as if he's some nervous animal that might skitter away at the first loud noise. "You being here. I didn't think you'd ever step foot in a Hopeful camp ever again."

"That was the plan."

"Thank you. For getting this back. I'd say I can't believe you pulled this off, but I know you too well."

Sebastian grunts. Not in agreement. Not in disagreement. It's only a sound, the minimal offering of a response.

A dull ache makes him aware of how hard he's clenching his teeth. With effort, he loosens his jaw. He pulls his hands from his pockets and crosses his arms. Glances once more toward the exit.

When he turns back to her, she looks away, caught watching him. She clears her throat and stares down at her prosthetic arm as if it's the most riveting thing she's ever seen.

"That's new." Her finger traces the black symbol on the back of the cybernetic hand.

"Bestowed by the Bandit Queen herself," Sebastian mutters, glaring at the broadside of the neighboring tent, not seeing it. "You ain't gotta worry about that being stolen ever again. Whole camp's protected as long as you flash that thing."

"Praise the Lord! Look at how God takes a hard situation and transforms it into a blessing."

"It wasn't some—" He bites back his sharp response.

He didn't come to argue, and he didn't come to get angry.

Why is he still here?

He lets out a slow breath that does nothing to ease the tension in his body. "Ain't nothing magical or divine about it. I went through a lot of trouble for your 'blessing.'"

"I didn't mean it like that. People can be blessings too. Even if they don't know it."

"Sure." Sebastian barely manages not to roll his eyes.

They lapse into a silence filled with all the things that aren't being said.

Things used to be easy between them. There was a time when they had almost nothing they couldn't say to each other. Or when no words were needed. He didn't have to admit that he couldn't stand lying alone at night. She'd just pull back the covers of her bed, sharing her warmth until the sun chased away the dark.

Now, all the unspoken things are a living creature. It swims through the air between them, keeping them well apart.

Sebastian uncrosses his arms again, straightens his shirt.

He should go. He's done what he came here to do. There's no reason to linger.

"I'm grateful for this." She pats the cybernetic arm. "But you never owed me anything."

He does roll his eyes this time.

She adds, "Except maybe a goodbye."

When Grace left Sebastian to rejoin the Congregation of Hope, she hadn't asked him if he was okay with it. She told him she was going back. That was that.

When she'd asked him if he'd come with her, he'd laughed. A short, incredulous, "ha!" that held no amusement.

Had his reaction shocked her?

In all the time that it was just the two of them, she continued to wear that one string of blue and white faith beads around her neck every single day. They were a part of her. He'd begun to resent the sight of them.

She prayed every night before bed and at the start of every meal. Sebastian rolled his eyes each time.

When she lost herself in the study of scriptures, he'd blast his music loud enough to be heard on the other side of town.

The morning after she asked him to go with her, he was gone before she woke.

No. His reaction couldn't have been a shock to her.

Her decision had been one she'd put off from the moment she became the one person who meant everything to him.

She'd known what his answer would be.

Same as he knows her answer before asking, finally, in a voice soft as the wind, "Come with me, Grace."

"Sebastian—"

"You coulda gone anywhere, Grace, and I woulda gone with you. Anywhere but this place."

"I know."

"I don't want it to be like this between us."

"You think I do?"

"Then let's go. Now."

She lets out a slow breath, heavy with sorrow.

Sebastian takes a step toward her. Just one. "Please."

"I can't," she says.

"Can't? Looks like you got two working legs to me. Maybe even a brain up there, despite all evidence to the contrary."

She gives him that too-familiar look of warning.

"You got a brain," Sebastian concedes. "I want you to use it."

"Still don't know how to apologize."

"Still ain't answered."

"I did."

"That one obviously don't count."

A smile breaks her stern expression. She chuckles, shaking her head.

He can still make her laugh. That's something, right?

When they lapse into silence again, it still sucks. But maybe it's slightly—only slightly—less uncomfortable.

"You know this was a goodbye gift, right?" she says abruptly.

"What?"

Grace pats the cybernetic arm, still on the table. "Knew it from the day you first gave it to me. It was your way of saying goodbye."

"I never said a thing about leaving."

"Didn't have to. I could see you didn't need me anymore."

"Don't you dare try to blame any of this on me," Sebastian says. "I wasn't going nowhere."

"You ran off to explore an Intelli-City all on your own. You were gone for days without even telling me where you went! You know how worried I was about you?"

"I came back! And I was able to do something for you."

"I didn't ask you to."

"When it's for somebody you care about, you just do it."

"When you care about somebody, you respect their choices."

"Unless they're being a moron!"

"Don't call me a—"

"You're gonna die here! Just like your dad."

"Just like your parents," she fires back.

Her words hit him harder than expected. His mother and father are ancient history. Their faces are blurry in his memory, their voices gone. Most details about them have been washed away thanks to a winning combination of losing them too young and the passage of ever more time.

This had always been the one topic off-limits between him and Grace. They never talked about what happened to them, what happened to everyone at the camp where his parents had been preacher and first lady.

The young kids taken. Everyone else killed. All but two lucky survivors.

"My dad," Grace says, gently. "Your parents. They didn't die for nothing. They believed in everything the Congregation of Hope does, and so do I."

"And my little sister. She deserved to be carried off by them things because of these stupid beliefs?"

"Of course not. You know that ain't what I'm saying. I get that this is hard for you—"

"And I don't get why it ain't for you. After everything that happened, you came back to the Congregation like it wasn't nothing."

"This life was always calling to me. And something different was calling you. That's okay."

"How is any of this okay?" He sweeps his arm wide. "For all you know, this camp already done picked up a dozen flatliners!"

That catches everyone's attention. Up to this point, the Hopefuls around them had been politely not noticing the argument flaring up between Sebastian and Grace. Now, they stop pretending they aren't following every word. They stare openly. Nervousness ripples through the onlookers.

"Oh, does that bother y'all?" Sebastian turns away from Grace and addresses the watchers. As ever, he obliges an attentive audience with a performance. "You think it, whisper it, make-believe like they can't possibly be here. But hearing their name out loud gets under your skin, don't it?"

A curly-haired woman grabs a boy gaping at Sebastian and drags him farther into the camp.

"Guess what?" Sebastian continues. "It bothers me too. I suppose watching flatliners massacre everybody you know has that kind of a lasting effect on a guy. It's only a matter of time before they strike again. You all know as well as I do that it'll happen in some place like this. Maybe even this very camp. Y'all really okay with that? And I guess you'd all be okay with the only family you got left in the entire world lining up for the slaughter!"

Grace snatches him by the arm, forces him to face her again. She's so close that she dominates his vision.

"Look at you!" she says. "Sebastian Yun don't get his way so he throws a tantrum. You ain't changed. The same self-centered little boy you always been. Guess that's my own fault. I put up with it when you were little. I figured it was the only way you knew how to work through what you suffered. But you know what?

"I suffered the same thing. I was there too! I was a kid too! And I stayed away from the Congregation for years because I knew how you felt about them, that you'd never come back with me."

"I never asked you to do any of that."

"What was I supposed to do? Leave a broken, bitter eight year old to fend for himself? Force him to return to the people he blamed for the worst day of his life? Or maybe I was supposed to leave him to die with the rest of our camp."

"What do you want? A medal? A statue? A hug? Is that what it'll take for you to stop being mad at me and get your ass on my bus?"

"I ain't mad at you. You're the one angry at the whole world."

"I'm the jolliest guy you'll ever meet."

"You still ain't made peace with what happened to us, and that's fine. Take all the time you need. But the world don't revolve around you, Sebastian. And neither do I. Not anymore."

"You really believe what these people do here is worth your life?"

"Yes."

Nodding, Sebastian pushes her hand off his arm. "Do

what you gotta do, Grace. But I can't lose another sister to them. I won't. If you stay here, that's it for us. We ain't family no more."

Grace opens her mouth to say something but clamps it shut again.

They stare each other down. The distance between them is shorter than when this all began, and so much bigger. Each watches for an indication—a hint—that the other will take back the truthful things that were said.

Maybe something in those years when it was just the two of them will be enough to crack through the massive wall erected between them.

Maybe it'll be those days of trekking across the hot, unforgiving wasteland, feeling like they were the last two people left in the world.

Maybe it'll be those long nights when a twelve-year-old girl held a little boy who was too scared to fall asleep, and how it was her arms around him that made him feel like he could finally close his eyes.

Maybe it'll be that moment when his new big sister fell over with laughter after something the little boy said, and he realized that he had this amazing power to bring light into her dreary world.

But no, this is it. The last time they'll see each other. And that shouting match was the last conversation they'll ever have. Because both remain silent.

Even as Sebastian turns to leave, neither says a word.

12

SEBASTIAN, Meza, Scott Buddy, and Betty the Cybernetic Arm follow Ruthless and her small army backstage. They come out on the reverse side of the backdrop and continue until they're surrounded by the bikes, cars, and trucks in various states of disrepair.

The fighting hasn't spilled into this part of the deck yet, but the noise of the clashes reminds them that as isolated as the vehicle graveyard might seem, they're not far removed from the violence. Her thugs spread out, covering the perimeter. Most face outward, but a few remain close, weapons pointed at the small trio.

"Um…" Sebastian faces the blank wall that is the Bandit Queen. "Sorry, Your Highness Ms. McTaggert, ma'am. Didn't mean to go and cause your big event to erupt into a ginormous riot."

She shrugs. "All our gatherings end like this. Why do you think I hold this summit only once a year?"

"Catering costs?"

She extends her hand, palm open and expecting. "The arm."

Stepping in front of Scott Buddy, Sebastian blocks monster boy and Betty from Ruthless. "That's ours. We won it fair and square. So if you think we're gonna hand it over after all we went through to get it, you can shove it."

Her hazel eyes drill into Sebastian with a stare cold enough to freeze his spine.

"Please and thank you, ma'am," he adds.

"I agree," she says at last. "The arm is yours. You will walk away with it today. But do not make me ask to see it twice."

"If we're gonna be walking away with it, how about we start moving our feet now?"

"You seem to be under the mistaken impression that my patience is endless."

One of the Black Raven thugs shifts his weapon, emphasizing that Sebastian isn't exactly in a position to question Ruthless's motives.

Sebastian moves aside, nods at Scott Buddy to hand the arm over.

Ruthless barely glances at Betty before passing it off to one of her lackeys, who carries it to a workbench several feet behind Ruthless. A second lackey is waiting. Together, they go to work on the arm.

"Hey!" Sebastian moves toward the workbench. "What're you doing to it?"

A tall Black Raven blocks his path.

"Whoever you've gone through all of this for must be someone special," Ruthless says.

"And?" Sebastian asks.

"You love her," Ruthless says, but she's looking thoughtfully at Meza when she adds, "but not romantically."

"She drives me crazy."

"Family is hard. I don't know if it's always been that way or if it's a reflection of these times we're living in. Tell me, which do you think it is?"

In the very near distance, the sounds of chaos and fighting continue, but here the Bandit Queen is shooting the breeze as if they're all chatting over porcelain cups of hot tea.

"Little bit of both, I guess," Sebastian says cautiously, sure she's laying the groundwork for some trap.

She considers his answer a moment before continuing.

"Sweetie and her brother ain't finished growing into the leaders I know they'll become. But they've done well so far."

"Uh…" Sebastian puzzles over the left turn in the conversation. And is that pride he hears in her voice? "You want them and their faction to get stronger? That don't make no sense. Even if all you bandit bosses secretly get together every year to hold hands and sing 'Kumbaya' by a campfire, you're obviously the top dog. You can't really want the young upstarts to threaten that."

"Can't I want my children to inherit the empire I've built?"

And suddenly, he sees it. Those are the same hazel eyes he'd been up close and personal with not too long ago. But they'd stared out from another face. Younger, with brown skin and a perpetual smile.

"Hawk took to fatherhood so effortlessly," Ruthless says. "They were his pride and joy from day one. I always said I didn't have the time or temperament for children. Wouldn't know what to do with 'em even if I'd wanted any. I chose to believe our arrangement was for the best."

"Okay, wait—just… slow down," Sebastian says. "You gotta give a guy's mind time to recover after it's been blown. I made out with the Bandit *Princess*?"

Ruthless cocks an eyebrow.

"I mean, that ain't the point… And you know what? We didn't even—" Sebastian clears his throat. "Your daughter is not an object, ma'am."

"Those two never asked me for help. So determined to do

things the hard way. Like their father. Or maybe that's how much they resented me for never being around."

"Maybe they didn't know it was an option."

She nods. "Whatever the case, by the time I heard what happened, they were already in the wind. They came back strong, though. Carried out what I woulda if the code I authored didn't prevent me from interfering with internal crew matters. But I know the challenges those two face now, and still, they refuse my offers to aid them.

"Then you introduced us all to these strange Old World contests. Everyone was surprisingly receptive to the idea of adopting them this year in place of our usual entertainment. Enthusiastic, even."

Ruthless's lackey shuffles back to her side and hands over Betty.

"This woulda gone a long way toward giving them a much-needed financial boost," she says, examining the arm. "Sweetie has always had such a powerful voice, even as a little thing. I hear that's how she and her brother made their way through the Feudlands. I'll hafta find other ways to help her and Razor without them knowing."

"Who's Razor?"

"Razor is the name I gave my son."

"Oh yeah. That makes so much more sense."

"Sweetie is very much like her father, but Razor must suspect he's more like me than he'd care to admit. 'Tom' is his rebellion."

"I get it. I went through a mohawk phase."

"This is yours." She extends Betty.

Sebastian grabs it even as he asks, "Why're you being so nice?"

"As you said, your friend here won it fair and square."

"That's the Black Raven mark." Sebastian notes the new

addition emblazoned on the back of the hand. "This here's your protection, ain't it? That's more than fair and square."

"Honesty is something I value but get far too little of. For some reason, most people I interact with have a difficult time relaying hard truths to me."

"Imagine that."

"So I reward it when I come across it. Still, I reckon I enjoy singing. I will continue to do it, and my men will continue to endure it." She smirks. It's a small and probably rare thing tinged with wicked humor. Again, Sebastian sees a bit of Sweetie in this woman.

"Be well, Sebastian. Whoever you are..." She gives Scott Buddy a clipped nod of acknowledgment. "I hope you find home again. And Meza, remember our conversation."

"Whoa, now!" Sebastian shifts toward Meza. He has a strange urge to throw her over his shoulder and run all the way to HRM. "Don't go trying to poach my people right in front of me."

"We spoke of other things," Ruthless says simply.

Sebastian arches an eyebrow. "Color me intrigued."

"Mind your business," Meza says.

"Pssh. I wasn't even gonna ask."

Ruthless turns, offering a dismissive wave as she strides back toward the fighting. "My men will return your weapons and see you out."

"Hey," Sebastian calls before she gets too far. "You really think you can fix what's broken between you and your kids?"

"I done made a lot of mistakes with my family. Maybe I don't deserve it, but yes. After all, what's life without hope?"

SEBASTIAN DRIVES FOR HOURS.

Away from Grace and Betty the Cybernetic Arm, the blue

flags, and the past. He drives until the sun is sinking into the horizon and Meza says, gently, "We gotta stop."

It's the first either of them has said since they returned to Her Royal Majesty.

Meza had been there. In the camp. He didn't realize it until he was storming away and caught sight of her, frozen and speechless at the edge of the small crowd of witnesses.

He isn't sure how much of his shining moment she caught. How much she heard. She'd known some stuff about his past. Bits and pieces. Maybe now she knows it all. He doesn't have the emotional bandwidth just now to decide whether he cares or not.

It's not like he's been purposely hiding his past, but few things bring down a room like pulling tragic backstories out of the dark, dank closets where they belong. Besides, these days, everybody has devastation in their past. His doesn't make him special.

He pulls the bus off the road, cuts the engine. HRM trembles as the current generators shut off and its frame settles onto the parking legs. Meza hits a button on the console. The metal shutters slide over the windows, providing an extra layer of protection against the night.

Neither of them turn on the interior lights. The glow from the console gives their silhouettes soft edges of green and blue.

"Sorry," Meza's silhouette says.

"For what?"

"Didn't know." She swallows. "Didn't know what the Congregation of Hope meant for you. That that's where—"

"How would you have known?"

"Coulda told me. You can tell me anything."

"I reckon we could pass the bottle back and forth and relive the worst moments of our lives together. Anything you've been dying to tell me?"

"I..." Her silhouette shifts, turning away from him.

Sebastian leans back in his seat. Sighing, he runs a hand over his face.

"If you had known," he says after a moment, "would you have kept on driving past that town like I asked?"

"No. Needed supplies."

"Well, there you go. Nothing to apologize for."

"Sure, but maybe I woulda been a little nicer about it."

Sebastian snickers. Then falls over the steering wheel, laughing.

"I mean it, jackass!" Meza snaps, not too nicely at all.

"I know, I know." Sebastian huffs, struggling to breathe. "Is that what it takes for you to be nice to me? And all this time, I just been a wondering."

Meza flicks on the lights. Probably so he can see her lethal glare.

"Glad you're feeling better." Only, the way she says it leaves him doubting her sincerity. "Night."

"Nooo!" Sebastian cries, following her down the aisle then up the stairs and to the top deck. "Don't stop being nice to me! Please? I'm a tortured soul. Pity me! Pity meeeee!"

She takes the immediate left at the top of the stairs and sweeps into her room. She slams her door in his face.

Sebastian stands alone in the aisle. His amusement fades slowly until he forgets what he found so funny.

"Night, Meza," he says soberly and moves toward his own room on the opposite end of the bus.

Passing the rows of bunks lining the aisle, he starts at a shuffling sound. It comes from the only berth with the curtain drawn tight. Scott Buddy has been holed up in there all day. Maybe the two of them had an overdue heart-to-heart.

Sebastian continues past the occupied bunk and makes it

all the way to his doorway before turning around and marching back.

He knocks on the frame of Scott Buddy's berth.

A messy blond head pokes out from the top bunk. "Sebastian Yun! Hello!"

"Buddy?"

It nods. "We are giving Scott break. Like Sebastian Yun is saying. Sebastian Yun is wanting Scott?"

"No. I wanna talk to you, actually."

"Oh."

"Yeah, I'm a little surprised myself."

"Why is Sebastian Yun talking to this Control?"

"Singing like you did back with the bandits, that something you sludges do? Y'all have nightly sing-alongs back in your hive or what?"

"No. Control are not making music."

"Then how'd you know you could do that?"

"When we are with Harmony, this Control is thinking always how to make Scott happy. Even when we are being secret. Then we are discovering Sebastian Yun's show and music. We are sneaking out far, far. Where no one is hearing. We are singing. Very loud. Song after song. Scott is happy. Very." It pauses, thinking. Or maybe remembering. "We are thanking Sebastian Yun for music."

"Huh" is all Sebastian can think to say.

Buddy blinks down at Sebastian. Waiting. Patient. So inhuman even in how it cocks its head.

"What do you prefer to be called?" Sebastian asks on impulse. "Not you and Scott. Just you. The sludge part. It? He? She? They?"

"Yes." Blink, blink.

"That ain't…" Sebastian lets out a sigh, mutters, "helpful."

The creature can't even wrap its brain around words like "I" and "you." Sebastian isn't shocked that it doesn't have much of a concept of personal identity in the most general sense.

"Never mind, Buddy. We'll figure it out later."

Buddy lifts its chin. "Yes. Yes. We are figuring."

"That's all, I guess. Night."

"This is being nice," it calls as Sebastian continues toward his room. "We are liking talking to Sebastian Yun."

"Sure."

In his room, Sebastian collapses on his bed and stares at the ceiling. He gives his brain about ten seconds to wander wherever it wants before deciding that's a very bad idea.

He activates his data cuff's screen and starts a broadcast as he pulls up the song he needs to play.

"I know you missed me, loyal listeners. Sorry I disappeared for a couple of days there, but I'm back. I always come back, don't I? Coming up, a song some of you might need right now, 'Wheel in the Sky' by Journey. A little reminder that tomorrow's gonna keep right on coming. Can't tell you if it's gonna be better or worse. Can't even guarantee that you or I will be there to see it. But sometimes, knowing it's there, that's gotta be enough."

Shutting his eyes, Sebastian lies back on his bed and lets the song carry him away.

THE STORY BEHIND THE STORY

I can't tell you exactly where the idea of singing bandits came from.

I'm pretty sure this book started out as "Sebastian has to steal something from some bandits." And somewhere along the line I thought, what if the bandits are doing karaoke when he breaks into their hideout? And somehow karaoke became an American Idol-inspired singing competition.

But why is this book non-linear?

I don't know. Cuz I'm weird. Whaddya want me to say?

I love nonlinear storytelling. I thought I invented it when I wrote my first backward story way back in high school. Then I read Kurt Vonnegut's *Slaughterhouse-Five*. Turned out I did not event that particular form of storytelling. My disappointment was tempered by how much I loved that book.

So maybe the story turned out nonlinear because it's a form of storytelling I gravitate toward.

I'm what you would call an intuitive writer. If a decision I make in my story feels right, I roll with it. If something I'm writing feels off, I get rid of it.

So maybe the story turned out nonlinear because it felt right.

Either of those reasons would be good enough for me, but fortunately I have had time to reflect on the question and get to the bottom of why my subconscious insisted that I tell the story in this way.

Sebastian is an avoider. Specifically, he avoids anything emotionally challenging. It's why he makes so many jokes.

His painful past is the last thing he wants to think about. And so the book avoids going there as long as it can.

I mean, it makes sense to me so let's just go with it, yeah?

Nonlinear storytelling was a risky move. I was pretty nervous to release this book, knowing that between the storytelling choice and the singing bandits, it may be the weirdest book in the series.

But on the plus side, I'd know that anyone who keeps reading after Book 2 is my kind of people. My kind of weird.

So thanks for being my kind of weird!

Music is clearly an important part of this series. It's sort of always in the background. But in this book, it was front and center. Choosing which songs each character would sing was not a task I took lightly. Particularly when it came to the song Buddy would sing.

The decision came down to three songs. "Can't Find My Way Home" by Blind Faith (particularly a cover by *The Voice* contestant Ryan Quinn, "The Real Folks Blues" by The Seatbelts (aka the Cowboy Bebop band), and "Wheel in the Sky" by Journey.

With its imagery of traveling on the road and hope of someday returning home, "Wheel in the Sky" won out, but all three of these songs evoked the feelings of longing and loneliness that tapped into what Buddy was feeling after the reality of never being able to return home landed.

I didn't want to skip over that feeling, and not only

because it's true to what that character was going through in that moment.

Singing this song, Buddy expresses an emotion that deeply resonates with Sebastian and challenges his assumptions about what a monster is capable of feeling. Which makes Sebastian very uncomfortable, and I'm in the business of nudging my characters out of their comfort zones.

So much so that I sometimes cackle to myself as I think about the things that are coming up for Sebastian, Meza, and Scott Buddy.

K.C. Cordell
    California, November 2024

WHAT'S NEXT? POST-APOCALYPTIC DJ: BOOK 3!

GRAB THE NEXT BOOK NOW AT WWW.KCCORDELL.COM/BOOKS

Here's your sneak peak at Sebastian, Meza, and Scott's next adventure: *So You're Teaming Up with a Creature of Evil (Post-Apocalyptic DJ: Book 3)*

"Later, when they murder us to death and proceed to use our skin as soothing face masks," Sebastian says as he, Meza, and Scott Buddy file out of Her Royal Majesty, "I want you to reflect back on the moment when I told you that this is a terrible idea."

He turns to HRM, gently butts his forehead against her rough, warm side.

"My liege," he coos, "you are but moments away from being stolen away from me. No. No, don't cry. We done had a good run. I will never forget you, and it is my hope that you will remember me fondly through the pain of our separation.

For though you will have been taken from me too soon, you will always hold a special place in my heart."

"Quit being dramatic," Meza says, starting toward the other vehicle.

"Let me drink in your grandeur one last time, Your Excellency!" Sebastian steps back to take in the entirety of the bus.

After his recent run-in with bandits and their enthusiastically dolled-up rides, he found himself thinking that HRM could use a little more zhuzh, as befitting the Queen of the Road.

Her dark-blue paint job had always given her a sleek appearance despite her size, but at the last town they stopped at, Sebastian bartered for some paint, blasted his music, and went to work. A few townsfolk joined in, then more and more. Some had surprising artistic acumen. Some were barely old enough to hold a brush. Now the bottom half of HRM is an energetic—if maybe slightly schizophrenic— mishmash of imaginative efforts. And it's absolute perfection.

Sebastian blows HRM one last sorrowful kiss. "I will love you forever!"

Before following Meza, he double-checks that he's locked the bus up tight. No reason to make it easy for these strangers.

In their distinct armor and helmets, the four gathered next to their enormous black truck are a tough-looking bunch. But the same can be said about everyone in the Midlands. Even tiny, little babies pop into the world already equipped with tension in their shoulders, permanently furrowed brows, and that weary, always-vigilant look in their eyes.

As Sebastian, Meza, and Buddy cautiously walk forward, the strangers make no move away from their vehicle. No weapons are drawn on either side, but holstered blasters are on full display. Not to mention the blades that the strangers carry. One of them has an especially humongous sword sticking out from behind his back.

Buddy curls Scott's lip up in a condescending smirk. "Look at silly humans. They are thinking they can hunt monsters."

Monster hunters have a very distinct style, making them instantly recognizable. Why they insist on piling on so much fur and feathers and leather in defiance of the relentless sun remains a mystery. Looking cool is one thing. And a thing Sebastian can get behind. In fact, he tried a similar style not too long ago. Sure, he looked like a badass, but at the end of the day, he'd prefer not needlessly sweating like a dog every day of his life. It's a bit extreme, as far as fashion choices go.

To top it all off, they sport full-face helmets that, like their armor, incorporate parts of slain hellions. They wear their helmets pretty much all the time. And that's why Sebastian has addressed every hunter he's ever met as Mando.

They never get it.

Then again, most of his top-tier references go over everyone's heads. To be fair, they are throwbacks to centuries-old pop culture, lost—it seems—to everyone but Sebastian, who consumes Old World content like it's The Stuff. Enough is never enough.

"Scared?" Sebastian taunts Buddy.

"Weak humans are never scaring this Control. Humans are slow. Clumsy. Very loud. Always. They are not hunting anything."

"Say it louder so the maybe monster hunters hear you. Actually, that's an amazing idea. Why don't you pop on over there and monster out? If they kill you in under thirty seconds, we'll know they ain't imposters with a plan to steal everything we got and murder us to death."

Huffing its horrible laugh, Buddy puffs Scott's chest. "We are wanting them to try."

"Hush up, both of you," Meza says. "They ain't hunting or murdering nobody. Gonna help 'em fix that truck. Then we go our separate ways."

Sebastian and Buddy flanking her on each side, Meza stops with a wide shouting distance left between them and the armored truck. The strangers' long, black shadows reach across the flat divide. Sebastian scrutinizes the getups of these supposed monster hunters. There'd be a benefit to grifters taking on these disguises.

Most folks like hunters. Midlanders may not get the warrior nomads and their wacky habit of chasing trouble, but no one disapproves of their proclaimed mission to rid the land of the monsters that prey on mankind. Because everyone agrees on one thing—the fewer monsters out there, the better. Except maybe those monsters who prey on mankind. They probably have a tough time getting behind the basic concept of monster hunters.

Sebastian shouts across the thirty feet of dry, cracked road. "I like your plumage!"

The strangers exchange looks, shaking their heads and shrugging.

Sebastian points to one of the guys. The shirt beneath his metal breastplate is topped with a wild assortment of feathers. They crowd his neck like a lion's mane. Sebastian gestures around his own neck to indicate that, obviously, that's what he meant. "It's very nice."

"Must you?" Meza says.

"What? Might as well start our bamboozlement on a good foot. And it *is* really impressive plumage."

Disregarding him, Meza calls across the distance, "I can help you with that vehicle."

"You don't even know what the problem is," a woman

shouts back. She has a bone motif going for her. Her helmet is framed by huge jaws that formerly belonged to some creature with impressive fangs. Smaller bones artfully march up across her breastplate.

"Don't change the fact that I can help," Meza says.

Sebastian shrugs. "But if you'd rather we mind our business and skedaddle, we are more than happy to oblige."

"I know that voice." It's the guy with the huge sword across his back. Brown fur, including a swath of pelts wrapped around his middle, accentuates the metal bits of his armor.

"Of course you do." Though he'd prefer to think that only cool people listen to his show, Sebastian is no longer surprised when sketchy types know his voice. It is merely a reality of his life as the Midlands' only celebrity that his reputation precedes him everywhere he goes. Being a Very Big Deal is the gift that keeps on giving. It turns out that being famous opens all sorts of doors, into both towns and hearts.

Maybe after these strangers reveal their nefarious plot, he'll be able to use his VIP status to get himself and Meza out of this mess. If it worked—well, sort of—with bandits, why not here?

"*So You Survived the End of the World*," the furry guy says.

Recognition flickers through the rest of the strangers. Some of the tension eases from their shoulders. Hands drop from their resting places on blaster handles and sword hilts.

Meza rolls her eyes. She has yet to learn how to appreciate the adoration that comes with being a part of the Midlands' favorite, and only, radio broadcast.

The Furry's face is full of awe when he says, "Guys, that's—"

"Please, please," Sebastian says. "No need to make meeting

your idol live and in person a whole thing. I'm a normal guy just like—"

"Meza!"

"—anybody else… Wait. Meza?"

The Furry pulls off his helmet and shakes out dark hair that falls around his eyes in soft curls. He appears to be somewhere around a similar age as Meza and Sebastian's seventeen and eighteen, respectively. He takes a step forward but stops, bouncing on his toes as if eager to close the big gap between them.

"I can't believe it," he says. "You're *the* Meza! We listen to your show every single day. This is amazing."

Sebastian squints at this blasphemer. "Her show?"

"Oh." The Furry barely spares a nod toward Sebastian. "And Sebastian Yun, of course."

Sebastian expects another eye roll from Meza, or for her to stare down this guy with a bland expression, or some other show of her usual impatience for this sort of thing.

But her scowl is deeper than ever, her eyes trained on the ground. "Want help with your vehicle or what?"

"We'd be stupid to say no." The Furry's smile is so wide Sebastian can practically count every tooth, even from this distance. "You're the best tech head out there. Reckon everybody knows that. I'm Riley, by the way."

"Then let's get on with it." Meza's eyes remain glued to the road.

"Hmm." As he watches her, Sebastian's curiosity is piqued. He shifts closer and bends over as if to examine the same spot of ground that's captured her rapt attention. "Something interesting happening down there, Meza?"

"Shut it, Sebastian."

Grinning, he straightens. Sure, they're most likely walking into a trap like a bunch of idiots, but how could he let her odd behavior pass without comment?

"First, some ground rules," he says, raising his voice again to reach Riley and the other so-called monster hunters. "I always appreciate running into adoring fans, but past experience has taught me that you enjoying my show and lavishing me with well-deserved praise don't mean I can trust you."

"No one is praising Sebastian Yun."

"Shut it, Buddy. So here's how this is gonna work. As long as you all don't try nothing, you'll drive away with a truck that runs better than what you started with. If any of you so much as twitch sorta funny, you won't be driving anywhere ever again. Cool?"

"And we're supposed to trust you with our vehicle?" says Bone Girl.

"As I said before, we're more than happy to mosey."

"No!" Riley says. "Please stay. We agree to your terms."

Sebastian takes a deep breath and lets it out. He ignores the rumbling in his ears, that now-too-familiar feeling of the asphalt crumbling somewhere behind him.

He'd rather the strangers refuse the help and give him a reason to drag Meza back to HRM. But they're really doing this.

So You're Teaming Up with a Creature of Evil (Post-Apocalyptic DJ: Book 3)

READ IT TODAY!

www.kccordell.com/books

SOMETHING AWESOME JUST FOR YOU!

Psst… Psst! Yeah, you! Want a free book?

Maybe you're craving more…

- Super fun, loveable characters
- That quirky humor you now know and love
- Larger-than-life monster action

Get your hands on K.C. Cordell's epic fantasy novella, *Destroying a World Eater for Beginners* for abso-freakin-lutely FREE when you sign up for her Newsletter of Awesomeness!

Visit:
www.kccordell.com/newsletter
and start reading today!

A WEIRDO HAS ABDUCTED YARI TO HIS CREEPY LAIR AND EXPECTS HER TO DO WHAT?!

SAVE THE WORLD, YOU PERV. GET YOUR HEAD OUT OF THE GUTTER AND START READING

Yari of Inera is a nobody. No. She's less than that. A mouthy orphan who gets by on her street smarts and nimble feet, she knows her place. So when she's plucked from her ordinary life and brought to an eerie, colorless fortress to be told by a man on a throne that she's some chosen one, she isn't impressed. She's seen her share of grifts and tricks. This one's no different.

Only her abductor's tricks defy her best attempts to explain them away. But stubborn to a fault, Yari will require solid evidence before she believes anything this strange man says about a world eater coming to destroy the planet. Or her being the one to stop it

Unfortunately for her, irrefutable proof is exactly what her abductor has in mind. Even if it puts her directly in the path of a cataclysmic disaster that she is nowhere near ready to take on…

If you like surly mentors, smart-mouthed chosen ones, and big monsters with even bigger appetites, then this gripping action and adventure fantasy is right up your alley!

www.kccordell.com/newsletter

MY SUPERSTARS!

To my family: Still putting up with me, eh? Heh. Suckers! ¬‿¬ (And also, thank you, I love you, okbye!)

To my readers: Kim, Carlitos, Clari, Rose, Abby, Willie, Abigail, Odessa, and Zoie. I appreciate you being the first to read this book. It's super cool of you to take your time and let me know what was and wasn't working for you in this book.

To Jay, Cherise, and Willie (again), and to the Queens of the Quill: It's an honor and pleasure to be in the trenches with you.

Thank you, Sara and Angela of Red Adept Editing and Nicole of Proof Before You Publish, for helping me give this book the ol' spitshine and polish. Let the record show that they did their best to stop me from breaking the English language too much. For all incidents of poetic grammar usage found within this book, blame me. And, also, those poetry classes I was forced to take in college. Everything is always poetry's fault…

To you, dear reader: Thanks for picking up this book and making it all the way through to the acknowledgements. You rock!

And a final thanks to Kurt Vonnegut. So it goes. When I was fourteen, I thought I invented non-linear storytelling. When I was seventeen, you informed me that I was mistaken. I had never been so happy to be proven wrong.

BTDUBS... WHO WROTE THIS BOOK ANYWAY?

L.A. native K.C. Cordell likes writing about aliens, monsters and superpowers. She attempted to write her first novel when she was nine. She didn't finish it, but it's still floating around. She read it recently. It's pretty good.

She likes reading and watching junk about aliens, monsters and superpowers too. Some of her favorite books and shows from growing up in the '90s include *Animorphs, Ella Enchanted, Gargoyles, Spiderman: The Animated Series,* and *Buffy the Vampire Slayer.* These inspired her to pick up a pen and their influence can still be seen in the writing she does today.

She hopes to one day own a t-shirt with an alpaca wearing an afro on it. If she ever got a puppy, she would name him Kiba. Thanks to once upon a time reading many, MANY books on the topic to her nephew, she's pretty good at pronouncing dinosaur names. Her favorite to say is pachycephalosaurus.

"Pachycephalosaurus."

Nice!

But she totally has to look up how to spell it.

Connect with K.C. on TikTok:
@bykccordell